Hollywood Sinners

Peter Joseph Swanson

StoneGarden.net Publishing

http://www.stonegarden.net

Hollywood Sinners Copyright © 2007 Peter Joseph Swanson

ISBN: 1-60076-041-4

StoneGarden.net Publishing
3851 Cottonwood Dr.
Danville, CA   94506

First StoneGarden.net Publishing paperback printing: February 2007

Visit StoneGarden.net Publishing on the web at
http://www.stonegarden.net

Dedicated to Tracy Hamby.

Chapter One

Karin scratched at the paint on some rotted wood as she looked out the narrow window of her basement apartment. She was thinking about the new invention that she'd just read about in her new March 1939 Look Magazine. It said, "Spun from coal". It claimed to be showing the very first pictures of a new sheer hose made from Nylon, a safe fiber already used in toothbrushes and fishing string, but for hose it was thinner than number 60 sewing thread.

"You need Nylon hose," Karin told the legs of the few women outside walking by. And she wanted them for herself, too, but she knew they'd be far too expensive. The ten-cent magazine had already used up the last of her piggybank. It was Monday and her husband wouldn't be getting anymore pay until Friday. So she'd also be skipping more meals.

Karin Panotchitch was sixteen and had already been married a year. Her twenty-seven year old husband worked at a shoe factory assembling cardboard boxes and it was a good enough job for the place and time. But then after work he went to the pool hall until late in the evening, spending most of his pay. He spent most of his weekends with his mother, who he said was always ill. Karin hated her marriage. She hated her husband's horrible jokes, bad breath, bad manners, and awkward last name. She was glad he was gone so much. She was glad that he'd probably forget that this day was their first year wedding anniversary. She assumed people were required to make whoopee with a spouse on a day like that. Karin was young, pretty and married, but she hadn't made whoopee in eight months.

She spotted a cockroach on her floor, chased it and lost. She sat back down on her musty sofa and began to bawl, feeling utterly sorry for herself. She finally fell asleep. She woke up hours later to the loud sound of her husband almost falling down the wood stairs, very drunk. Though he'd somehow kept upright when what was underfoot was uneven, when he got to the tiles he fell to his knees and then his side. He ordered, "I want some fried potatoes."

She had no food but she didn't admit it. Karin just said, "Rest. It'll be at least ten minutes."

"Stupid bitch!" He blindly crawled sideways towards the couch and missed it, hitting his head on the fieldstone wall. He yelled at her unintelligibly as he backed up and finally found the cushions. He started to loudly snore.

Karin took one of the firmer throw pillows and put it snuggly over his face. He didn't struggle for air. He just stopped breathing and died. Karin looked carefully at the pillow to see if he'd slobbered on it. It didn't seem like he had. She smiled and put it back and then went to bed. She had trouble sleeping. She tossed and turned and tried to not think. But she was so hungry, and a hot greasy fried potato with a bit of salt was all she thought about until morning.

When the sun came back and it was bright enough to read in the room, Karin began to study her Look Magazine again. She carefully turned the large pages so they wouldn't wear out. In the ads, a Plymouth Coupe went for 645 dollars and a Sedan for 685. She wondered how anyone could afford all that money. There was an article about U.S. Fascists but she didn't care about that. She went back to the page about the Nylon hose and she read about how the Nylon will soon supplant silk. The silk came from Japan and their economy would suffer, as Nylon would be made at home.

Karin was glad for that as she wondered where she could get a job making Nylon hose. She imagined a marvelous tall clean white factory with shiny silver machines of the most advanced design making musical purring sounds as it spun out fibers like cotton candy. She imagined herself surrounded by mountains of hose that smelled like a cross between new clean pencil erasers and hot sugar. She assumed she'd get complimentary pairs to wear and she could wear three pairs at a time if she so chose so her legs would look like those of a flawless china doll as she sat at her Nylon-making workstation.

She looked up at her dead grey husband and finally wondered what she should do about him. She frowned; he was still such a bother. On the sheep farm she grew up on, dead animals were just dumped in a back ditch. People were supposed to be worth more dignity than sheep. Sometimes.

* * * * *

She washed her face, dapped a little rouge on her lips from a tiny metal tin that was almost empty, and then went to the police station, and then to his mother who was supposed to be ill all the time. Karin looked down at the worn toes of her black shoes on the lush Oriental rug. She repeated what she'd told the coppers. "He's dead."

The old woman, sitting in a whimsical chair made from woven banana leaves, made a judgmental face. "Dead? That's horrible. Then who'll play cards with me come Sunday?"

"And Saturday," Karin reminded her. "He's gone here all day on Saturday, too."

The old woman looked at Karin as if she were stupid. "No, dear. Just Sunday. "I've never seen him on a Saturday."

Karin didn't look surprised. "Oh. That's where he told me he went. Because you were ill. Usually. Right?"

The old woman took a slow sip of her root beer from a paper straw, not seeming to care about how tasty it was. "Do I look ill? I've never been ill a day in my life. And if I was so ill, and you really thought that, why didn't you come and clean my house for me. That's what a real daughter-in-law does. She comes and makes herself useful."

Karin tried not to stare too much at the root beer; she wanted one so badly. "That's what he told me. You were ill. And he forbad me from coming with him."

"Why? That's a lie."

"He said you where his mother. You weren't mine."

The old woman made another bitter face. "My boy was a fancy pants liar. He lied to you about how old he was. He lied to me about what that money that I gave him was to be for – to buy you two a house. He lied that you was to have a baby. And you're a liar, too. A marriage of fancy pants liars. I bet you told him that lie. People like you and him will just say anything to get by from minute to minute without having to do any real work."

Karin began to weep. "I wanted a baby."

The old lady decided that her straw was getting soggy in her root beer so she replaced it with a fresh one. "Well I suppose you married him knowing you'd someday get my inheritance. I'm sure that's why he told you I was so ill all the time, to get you greedy so you'd have him. In my day a man had to at least take a bath to get married but nowadays it's just about greed. But you don't get a penny from me until I'm dead. If I'm good and dead by then, then I hope I won't have to hear about it. You aren't in my will by name and that not because I forgot about you. I remembered to leave you out. But I suppose the law would make sure you'd get what would have gone to him. The law is the law. Laws are socialism. I hate them all." She took another indifferent sip of her root beer.

Karin fainted. She hadn't thought about the will before. Such good news about a brighter future should have bolstered her spirits. But her blood was empty - she was too famished to stay on her feet a moment longer. The old woman let her lie where she'd fallen, and when Karin's eyes opened, she was told, "Get out, you lazy strumpet. You can lie in the street all you want like a drunken fool but I'll have none of that in here in my Christian home. Toodle-oo!"

Karin blurted, "You're the Devil! The Devil himself! That's who your are!"

"How dare you speak to me this way!"

"But it's true! An ugly old Devil, too!"

"You don't know anything about what you speak of. That just proves your ignorance!"

"I know plenty! The Devil gives things and makes promises and the Devil takes things away and breaks our hearts! And all that!"

The old woman corrected Karin by a quote from scripture. "It's the Lord that giveth and taketh away. Blessed be the name of the Lord. You ignoramus."

"It's the Devil! And the Devil is just like you!"

"And if you keep calling on the name of the Devil, he will appear in person and take you to way down to the stink of Hell bodily, so goodbye!"

Karin proudly stuck out her chin. "I ain't afraid of anybody. I ain't afraid of the Devil! I ain't afraid of you! I've known too many devils all my life and they ain't worth the bottom of the outhouse!" Karin wanted to murder the old woman with a stake through her heart so she could drink her root beer. But instead she went outside and stood in the street, in the cheery sun, and watched all the people go by, wondering what it was that made them go, until she fainted again.

* * * * *

She woke up in a big hospital room. There were nuns. One noticed her eyes open and so went to her. "You're at the NPP - a charity hospital. And you've still got both your arms and legs."

Karin looked around, confused. "Where am I?"

"The Nuns of Perpetual Patience." She smiled like it was a joke. "That was one of the virtues last time I checked. With girls like you, patience is just part of the ball game. Is this strike one for you? Or are you out?"

Karin saw her lips moving but had trouble stringing the words together. "What?"

"Wake up! Wake up! You're not dead so wake up. This ward is just for the ladies, so don't be shy. You were found like you were dead in the street. They couldn't find a pulse. You didn't even seem to be breathing. What a stunt. But you're not dead. Are you a wayward girl?"

"What's that?"

The nun smiled in relief. "Good that you don't know. You shouldn't know what that is. Then, what's wrong with you, dear? Do you know?"

"I fainted. I think. Not too kippy of me, huh?"

"Yes." The nun raised her exquisite eyebrows. "Do you know why you did such a thing?"

"I guess I haven't eaten."

The nun chuckled. "You silly skinny young girls and your diets. Did you skip breakfast again? Vanity vanity."

Karin began to weep.

"Oh? Oh. How long has it been since you've eaten?"

Karin couldn't exactly remember. She'd eaten all the bugs she could catch in the basement but she really didn't want to count those. "Last week there was a turnip I stole from Mrs. MacGutty's garden in the middle of the night. I'm such a sinner."

The nun turned to another nun and ordered her, "Oatmeal soup. No lard. If it's too rich this poor girl will just vomit it right back up. Keep it as plain as can be."

Karin noticed the same March issue of Look Magazine on a table near her. "Nylon stockings."

The nun regarded the magazine and added, "What a great issue. And there are Nazis in America! Jiminy Cricket!" The nun shook her head like it worried her, and then added, "Tell me about yourself? How did you come to this bad luck?"

"I grew up on a sheep farm."

"You don't sound like a country girl."

"I grew up in Montana. And anyway, Dad made me speak properly because he said I should become a secretary some day."

"That's nice work for a lady."

"But I've never touched a typewriter in my life. I know all about sheep though. More than I want. And I can drive a tractor."

"Oh?" The nun raised her eyebrows again and leaned forward a bit, encouraging her to talk.

"The farm was hard work, sure. It was so cold in the winter I thought I'd die. But the awful cold made the sheep grow thick long wool. We did good enough selling wool that we got the bills paid. That was better than most folks could say. The dust bowl didn't hit that far north so we didn't have any of those same troubles as the Okies. But I wanted to leave the farm. I wanted to go to

Hollywood."

"Hollywood! Oh my!"

Karin winced. "I know they say it's a sin city, but I don't care what they say. I have to see it for myself. It can't be all that bad, can it?"

The nun smiled. "I don't know if there really is such a thing as a sin city. Maybe Sodom and Gomorrah, but that was a little while ago."

"I heard of that." Karin's eyes widened. "Oh. They were the ones in the Bible that blew up because there was nobody decent in them. Right?" She smiled proudly for having some knowledge of the Bible in front of a nun. "There was fire and then there was salt. Or is that fire and brimstone?"

"All of it. You got the story pretty good. Now, why do you want to go to Hollywood? It fascinates you? It does seem fascinating, doesn't it? All those movies!"

Karin said, "Sure. I seen enough pictures of it in the magazines and it seemed like the best place to be in all the world and I wanted the best. I didn't see why not. Then Daddy died when the tractor went right over his head. And it wasn't even his tractor. We never owned one. Too much money. It was the neighbor's." Karin paused to remember finding him squished with his eyeballs and tongue hanging out. "It was terrible."

"I'm sure it was. You poor doll."

"The sheep were all sold off. I took my share of the money, split between me and my six brothers, and I got on a bus. But on the bus I met a man who was just coming this far. This is where his mother lived. He charmed me and like a fool I got off here with him. I didn't go to Hollywood. I got married and now he got so drunk he stopped breathing. So here I am."

"He stopped breathing?"

"He was blind drunk."

"Drunk?"

Karin nodded. "Too blind to breath!"

"Oh sweet Mary." The nun grabbed the Look Magazine. "I

was just thinking. On this page. Don't you think you look just like Jeanette MacDonald? I love her. She's such a darling canary."

Karin looked hard at it, and admitted, "With her mouth open like that, sure. But she has such tiny eyebrows."

The nun pointed between her own eyes. "If you shave that. All the stars do. They pluck. What they have isn't natural. They have to work hard to look like that."

Karin touched above her nose. "Really? Is that their secret?"

The nun nodded. "Tweezers. That's the start of looking like a star."

Karin finally noticed that the nun had well groomed eyebrows. "You do it?"

"Don't tell anyone. I may be a nun, but I still want to be glamorous, too. I go to the movies. When I saw Mae West's eyebrows I thought I'd cry, they were so beautiful."

"But isn't that a sin - to see one of her pictures?"

"Maybe it is. But maybe it isn't if you're just looking at the eyebrows." The nun pointed at the corner of the room at a colorful statue of Mary. "Her eyebrows are painted on."

Karin chuckled. "I'm sure."

The nun smiled big like she had just done something wrong, and then got up and left.

Karin asked the woman in bed next to her, "What's a wayward girl?"

"A streetwalker. You know what that is?"

"No."

"A bad girl. A girl who sells her basket of strawberries. A girl who hops in and out of cars of men she never met before and will never meet again. A girl who don't mind pitching woo for a quarter in the alley."

"Pitching woo for real dough?"

"Bingo. A good soda pop sucker. With a little hootch thrown in to make it a real ring-a-ding-ding." She winked. "You get my jazz?"

"Sure." Karin looked off, oddly. Since she was twelve her six older brothers had always made her pitch woo with them, they were all always so crazy to do it. She wondered if she should have been paid for it.

The woman looked at Karin with pity. "You beat?"

Karin put her nose in the air. "I may be poor, today, but I'm going to be a star."

"Then shoo. You should head off to an apple. Las Vegas ain't too far if you don't mind crawling through a lot of sand, first. If you can just get the hell out of Idaho. I think this place is a trap. Get out! Even to Las Vegas at first, if you can get that far. It's hot but there's a few buildings that do nothing but sin all day. There's some work for a lady willing to sell her honey cooler – and then you can make a few nickels to ride your keester all the rest of the way to Hollywood in style. It's always important to arrive in style."

Karin felt defensive. "Don't be all wet. I'll hit the parade in Hollywood. For sure. I'm going to get there if I have to thumb it."

"Halleluiah, sister."

"I mean it. And I'm not selling myself like that ever. I'll work at a flower shop, first. Or a candy shop. Or a notions counter in some drug store. I got my pride. But that's defeatist talk anyway. I'm going to be a star. I'll be the one having flowers and candy and pretty ribbons sent out to me in my dressing room - as my hair is being all done up like Norma Shearer."

"With cement and cellophane? She's a real pally, but I don't believe her for a minute. A person shouldn't try to smile so much while they talk. It's revolting."

Karin asked, "What do you think of Jeanette MacDonald?"

"She's an old piece of rock candy. She opens her mouth and I get cavities."

"What do you think of Hollywood? Is it really so scary? Is it wicked? Is it as terrible as some Bible city?"

The woman shrugged into her pillow. "Pfff. I'm sure it's like any place else. There's stupider people that you can take advantage of. Yeah them. And there's the smart people who'll take you for a pony ride, all the time. It's like that anywhere you go, I'm sure. Pretend to be palsy-walsy with some rich chiseler so he don't think to chisel you. Nope. Life is hard. Life ain't ever no Shangrila."

Karin made a smug expression. "Well, anyway, I'll be better than all of them. I'll show everybody in that mean town how to be nice."

"Don't knock it if you're not. Not at all. If you sell your rat-a-tat enough times then you know at least you'll have enough dough to wear a nice dress. If you get in the right circles then the money will just be rolling like barrels of monkeys. When that happens, you'll not only get three meals a day, but it'll be whatever you want. Until you pay the Reaper. But that happens to you anyway, even if you hide behind a notions counter your whole sorry life. The Reaper still comes. You don't have to live in Hollywood to see death."

Karin looked off in bliss as if she was having a celestial vision. "There is something always keen about the idea of a nice ten dollar dress."

"Ah yes, to be togged to the bricks." The woman sadly grimaced. "I'm just here because now I've been rotting away inside from more social diseases than I can throw a fat copper at." She winked again though she had started crying. She let the tears drop onto the side of her pillow. "Funny how you have to pay for that big juicy steak. And when I drop dead I hope the whole damn town drops dead with me."

"Do you have a tweezers?"

* * * * *

Thanks to the unconditional charity of the Catholic Church, Karin received two more meals of oatmeal, the second one even containing some lard. Then she went to a park and sat on a bench near a flagpole. She carefully opened the copy of Look Magazine that she'd filched from the nuns. Perusing the pages, she decided that she didn't care about the U.S. Nazis that had several of the most prominent articles. Rather, she was utterly fascinated by the cover story. 31 Hollywood Feuds. Connie Bennet stole Gloria Swanson's husband. Marlene Dietrich had said that she'd never heard of Mae

West, so Mae said she'd take her apart. Wallace Beery got mad at Mickey Rooney for overacting in their scenes together. There was a coolness between Shirley Temple's and Jane Withers' mothers over a tacky Temple impersonation. Laurel and Hardy suffered professional jealously. And the cover showed the giant color faces of Joan Crawford and Norma Shearer, since they were the biggest Hollywood catfight of them all, and for reasons beyond any one article.

Karin said to the park trees, "I'm going to be like them stars. And when I feud with them, I won't put up with anything. I'll even find a way to bump them all off if I have to, to get them out of my way. If it comes to that. I'll plug them all full of holes." She laughed at herself. "Why not? I deserve the best."

A woman walked up the sidewalk with her dog. The dog looked like a pair of sideways earmuffs on pencils for legs. She plopped down next to Karin. "Isn't that magazine just keen? So informative. I read that issue all afternoon yesterday and I've just been thinking about it all day long today. I was so troubled about all that anti-Nazi stuff. Did you see that yet?"

Karin recoiled, not liking someone like that sitting next to her like that. She gave the odd dog the meanest look she could. But then she just shook her head. "I don't know anything about those things. I'm just learning about all the Hollywood stars."

"Oh, they're marvelous, aren't they? Just marvelous. But look what that magazine says about women in Nazi Germany. It says right there on that page. That one showing the sweet German girl with the axe. Chopping wood. It says that they're taught only two things. To take care of their bodies so they can have lots of babies for the State. And to be loyal to National Socialism."

"Careful you don't tear the paper." And Karin decided to give the dog another dirty look.

"Well. What girls aren't expected to have babies for their country, and to be loyal to their country? We do that here. I'm sure they do the same thing anywhere. I bet even the Eskimos are expected to behave. And nobody would complain about that. Do Eskimos chop wood? Hmm. I wonder."

Karin looked off at the trees again and thought about how when her father had found out what her brothers were doing with her, catching three of them in the act all at once, he acted like that's what girls were for; to let boys who's bodies had gotten that old have pleasure. So he put her away under lock and key as if it was half her fault. When the tractor rolled over her father's head she was glad. She wished she'd thought of doing it to his head herself, somehow. He should have gotten a worse punishment, in her opinion, for not making sure that she was more special above all her brothers. There was only one way to do that now – to become more special than anybody else in the whole wide world – to become the greatest Hollywood star, ever. Then Karin realized the woman was still talking.

"And did you see how that paper, The American Protestant, thinks it's special somehow in being more American than anybody else? And that it can trash the Catholics like that as being un-American? But they are. I would suppose. They pray to bones."

"What?" Karin stated, "Nuns are aces."

"I suppose they are. Even if you're praying to bones all the time, at least you're still praying. That's better then the Reds."

Karin said, "Some nuns don't have much time to pray. They're to busy helping the sick. And feeding wayward women."

The woman suddenly looked at Karin like she might have tuberculosis. "You aren't one of those heathen Catholics, are you? If you are, I'm very sorry to have offended you, but I just don't see how praying to bones will get you to Heaven. So, as far as how I can figure, all Catholic are going to Hell."

"No. Of course I'm not a Catholic. I don't think so. It's been awhile since Daddy took us to church, and I don't even remember what kind it was. I was just a little girl and forgot to ask. I just don't want to be prejudiced against nuns. I admire purity and discipline, and people belonging to something bigger then themselves." Karin wished she somehow had some of those things for her own life. "So I don't think I'm a Catholic. I don't have anything."

"Good. None of them are getting into Heaven, praying to idols and all. But what does it matter to me." She absently patted her dog's head. "It's just gotten all too political, I agree. Just because you pray to bones really hasn't much to do with politics, I suppose. And did you see in that magazine how the American Fascists want to take the Leaning Tower of Pisa and save it from leaning and rebuild it in America and have it as its headquarters, here? You don't have to be in that political party to think that that'd be very good for American tourism. I'd go see it, that's for sure, if it were here. What a sight."

"A tower? Like the one in Babylon where everybody forgot English? I don't remember the story. I was only a little girl." Since Karin wasn't sure what all that meant, so she thought again about becoming a star. She wondered how one started out doing such a thing. Did the crackerjack dress come first or would she get a crackerjack dress because she already was the star. It was a chicken and egg issue, which came first, that put her mind into a loop of confusion.

"Oh, you're not listening to me, I'm such a bag of wind and I see you're so tired. I gotta go anyway and pick up some bones for the puppy. The butcher at the other end of the park, over there through those trees, just loves my poopsy-wooh. He's my baby." She got up. The dog lifted his leg and squirted Karin's.

"Hey!" Karin hit the dog on the head.

"I never!"

"Your dog is a smart-alec!"

The woman made some gasping noises and hurried away.

Karin sat awhile thinking and thinking as hard as she could. But she had trouble getting it to go anywhere. She thought about the sheep farm and how she had wanted to leave it so bad. Now she was gone from it. She thought about how selfish her brothers had been with her, and her husband in his own way, but now she only had herself to please. It didn't sound Christian for a woman to think that but she didn't care. "It's just me and my shadow. I'm going to Hollywood or bust! I don't care how sin city it is - I may just fit in."

Deciding that a magazine would be too much baggage, she left it behind on the park bench. She didn't need pictures of stars anymore;

she was going for the real thing. She walked to the road that led south out of town and from there thumbed a ride through the desert on the back of a truck transporting chickens. She got as far as the watering hole of Las Vegas, looked around at the dust blowing against the few small one room shacks, and when she saw a Mexican prostitute stagger out to a doorway to vomit on the doorstep, she decided that there was nothing she could see to stay for. Karin put out her thumb again. She got a ride from a woman in a big red car.

They sat side-by-side in silence. So Karin passed the time thinking about how she should have killed her mother-in-law. She wondered how she would have done it, to get away with it. She wondered how she could jump out of the car at every greasy spoon they passed and how she could eat something for free and still not loose her ride and keep going. She wondered if it would be a good idea to murder the woman driving her now and rob every greasy spoon somehow along the way, and then sell the car in Hollywood for enough money to pay room and board for a year.

Finally the woman said, "Oh, sorry to not be talkative - just thinking about my new business venture. I'm so excited to be going to L.A."

Karin asked, "You're not at all afraid, or worried in the least? Hollywood is there."

"Why? Of what? Of failing? I can do that anywhere. I might as well go to try my luck where there's people I can sell to. What did you mean?"

Karin said, "All the sinning and evil. Some say it's a sin city. Hollywood is."

She laughed. "People say all sorts of things. Yap, yap, yap. Well, it's nice to be talking to you, anyway. I bet you thought I was so rude to not say anything to you at first, as if I was mean or all high hat or something."

Karin assured her, "That's okay. I was just thinking, myself. I wasn't talking either. It takes two. I was just thinking about – about - how to become a star."

"Oh. That's about as scarce as a hen's tooth. Maybe worse. It's hard to be a star."

Karin nodded tensely. "I know. But I gotta, somehow."

"I'm Rita Sunshine. I'm going to L.A. to sell my special exclusive suntan lotion. I make it, myself, with a special mixture of olive oil, zinc, chamomile, and a dab of coconut oil so it smells like coconut cream pie and you just want to eat it. But please don't. Oh —and there's also coffee in the ingredients that's been ground super fine from a special electric machine."

"Oh my." Karin was most impressed. "An electric machine?" She wondered if it was anything like the elaborate contraption she'd once seen in a Betty Boop cartoon in the newspaper. It grabbed things and chewed them into something else. It had said that someday people could go shopping without having to leave their homes, thanks to such grabbing machines that would reach all the way to market.

Rita Sunshine continued, "Grinds it to dust. And I'll sell tins of it on the beach. That's what the whole back seat is full of. And my electric machine is in the trunk."

"Good luck."

"My every last penny is invested in my special lotion. Every last penny. So I'll need all the luck I can get. Luck and sunshine."

"Good luck to you and me both."

"Rita Sunshine. Remember my name. Rita Sunshine. Sunny L.A. is just waiting for me with open arms. I'm sure of it. I hope. You'll see me in every drugstore and beach everywhere. I'll go national like Marvelite."

"What's that?"

"Dress shields. Didn't you know the Marvelite brand? I just used that as an example because I'm wearing them now. I got to look cool as a cucumber in L.A. if I'm going to sell my Rita Sunshine suntan lotion, so I have lots of dress shields."

"Oh sure." Karin watched a billboard for Pebeco tooth powder go by. Smile Like a Star! "Sure. And we'll be big. Both of us! You and me both!"

Chapter Two

At the end of the line, when Rita Sunshine let Karin off at the bus station, she stood there awhile in confusion. Karin noticed red paint on the wall that read, The Fascists have crushed the Godless liberals in Spain - next the world. Praise God. And it was punctuated with a swastika.

"How radical!" Nobody would have done such a political and religious act where she'd come from – and such things were hardly even spoken of. She wiped the sweat off her forehead and went inside to look for a drinking font. When she found it, she drank desperately.

A handsome swarthy man in black shellacked hair stepped up to her. "Slow down. There's only so much water in the reservoir."

She took a deep noisy breath and looked up at him in alarm.

"Hello. I'm Ramon Classic. At your service."

"Oh?" She wiped her mouth. "Classic? Is that really your name?"

"No. It's just that I'm a classic. Ramon Classic."

Karin asked, "And what does Ramon mean?"

"That's my name. "Where's your bags? I'll help you carry your bags."

"I don't have any."

Ramon Classic said, "I thought you looked poor. Really beat, like you've just been barely hanging on by your eyebrows. You an Okie?"

"What?"

"From Oklahoma? A migrant. The town's flooded with them and they aren't wanted. But I don't care."

"I know what an Okie is. Everybody hates 'em." Karin eyed him suspiciously. "Where you from?"

"Chicago, originally. Me and all my brothers." He began to speak in an Irish accent. "In a part of town that irritated me dear Mother. We are from Sicily, really, and shouldn't be speakin' like this. Especially not to me dear Mother." He laughed. "He reverted to an Italian accent. "My Mama MIA! And we're all so confused. Are we Chicago gangsters? Are we Irish gangsters? Are we Sicilian gangsters? Or will this new home make us Hollywood gangsters? I think Hollywood sounds like the best place for gangsters. Don't you? Did you ever see Cagney in The Public Enemy? Rat-a-tat-tat!"

"No. I missed that one. The ticket cost money. And I'm not from Chicago, either." Karin explained, amused, "I'd have taken the train. But that mostly goes from east to west and I came down from up north."

"Canada?"

"Not that far."

He walked a slow circle around her. "No - you don't look poor because you're in a bus station, but because you don't have any bags. And your dress."

"What's wrong with my dress. It's kippy enough."

Ramon Classic made a slight condescending face. "It's a bit plain. That's all. Have you even eaten in the last year?"

"Why would you ask something like that?"

"You look like a rack of bones in that dress. You'd think you were a Hollywood star and you were getting yourself down to picture weight."

Karin looked down at her sinewy arms. "Picture weight?"

"All bones. So the camera sees your cheekbones and jaw. And so you're all peepers. And all that. But if you keep it up you'll just be a dancing skeleton."

"Well, I am going to be a star."

"Oh really. You know somebody?"

Karin looked down. "No. Do I have to?"

Ramon said, "It's a very good start. But it don't guarantee everything. They say lots of stars had brothers come to ride their coattails and they usually don't ride too far. You have a place out here set up to live?"

"Well. Not exactly."

Ramon smiled big. "You don't have a penny to your name. Do

you."

"Is that any of your concern? I think you're asking too many questions. Why are you asking all these questions? What do you want from me?"

"Dollface. Slow down."

"Well, I think it's a perfectly legitimate thing for a girl to ask a strange man about -- who's been talking to her like they're old friends."

Ramon put up his hands. "Slow down. I just saw you and greeted you."

"Are all men so nice in Hollywood?"

"No. But I'm nice to just you."

"Why?" She put her hand on her hip. "So you can murder me?"

"What?"

"Yep." Karin looked him up and down. "Are you an insane murderer?"

Ramon said, "You've been reading too many movie magazines."

Karin asked, "How can you tell? How can you read my mind?"

"Because that's where all the murder stories are printed. And most of them are all made up, I bet. There's probably no more murder here than anywhere else in the country. And really, there ain't much anywhere else, either, I bet. It's just that here it gets all the press for some reason. Well, ever since that woman was found all cut up into pieces and carved out like a pumpkin and then her hair was done, well I can see why a fuss was made! That was a nightmare out for everybody to see. But that don't happen everyday. I don't ever plan on being murdered. Punched out a few times, sure. But never murdered. You should go around thinking the same."

"What do you want from me, then?"

"You want to make some money with me? I'll make some money with you. I'll protect you while you're out there on those hungry streets. And I'll make sure you'll have a shoulder to cry on when your day is through."

She liked the looks of the shoulders of his suit jacket. "How?

Why?"

"You ever made whoppee with a man just for the money?"

Karin felt all the blood drain out of her face. She turned to leave him, and then fainted.

* * * * *

Karin woke up in a small room. It was almost as small as her bedroom on the sheep farm had been, and that was very small. "Where am I?"

Ramon got up from a stool. "Hey sweets. So you're not dead."

"Dead?"

Ramon said, "I couldn't even find your pulse. You weren't even breathing! I was mighty worried."

Karin's eyes started working. "You!"

"Ramon Classic at your service."

She sat up. "Why am I here? Where am I?"

"Los Angeles. Hollywood. Okay, I don't know exactly if it's Hollywood or just outside. I just know we're not in Beverly Hills. But we're somewhere. It's all the same pot of gold in a paper cup, out here. A bunch of suburbs in search of a city."

"What is this room?"

Ramon answered, "A boarding house. I'm renting a room at the back of the carriage house. It ain't a carriage house no more, of course. The main house is up front. That one's got the nicer rooms, and board. But I'm on a budget. But soon my brothers and I will rule this town. We have a plan."

"Where's my dress?"

"You look so sweet like that in your undies."

She pulled modestly on her slip. "Where am I?"

"My room. You fainted. You had to go somewhere. I collected you and took you here. Aren't I swell?"

"Why here?"

"Everybody has to be somewhere."

Karin gasped. "I've been kidnapped!"

"Nah, I ain't no frightner so don't look at me like that. I never laid a finger on ya!" He held one up.

Karin squinted at his finger. "It isn't that part of you that worries me."

"Ha. Ha. No. I never kidnapped you or anything else ungentlemanly like."

Karin looked around the small room. "I've been kidnapped!"

"Slow down. No you have not."

"Then why am I here? I don't know where I am! So I've been kidnapped!"

He asked, "And where would I send the ransom note for fifty dollars?"

She smiled at that, though she didn't want to. "So - you rescued me?"

"That's it. I'm your Lone Ranger."

"And want do you want from me? You want me to have made whoppee with you for money?"

"My. You operate fast. Slow down, dollface."

Karin said, "No. I just remember that's what you asked me before the lights went out."

"Let's slow down, muffin." He opened a can of corn. "Here. Eat this. It's not as good as Mama's meatballs with black olives all inside. Mmmmm. Mama's meatballs with black olives." He sadly gazed off in thought for a moment, and then added, "Eat good and slow so it digests well. And then we chew the fat."

She spooned in a small mouthful and then began to weep. "Ooooh! This is the most delicious thing I've ever eaten! Just snazzy! Oooooh!"

"Yes. It's the best. You should have the best, sometimes. Now no more talking, and eat it all down real slow. Chew it good or it won't digest."

When she finished the can, she asked again, "You want to make whoppee with me? I don't think so. I'm just not that kind of person."

"But you're beat."

"I'll get a job at a flower shop. Or a notions counter. Or I'll sell shoes."

Ramon laughed. "You'll be knocking on their doors for a month and you'll find that the only jobs that open up are picking oranges. You a farm girl?"

"Hell no!" she lied. "That's all wet!"

"Well then, if you want to make some dough in style, you got to work the streets."

Karin said, "I think I'll work in a perfume shop until I become a star."

"You have to wait in line behind a hundred other girls just like you just to be told they ain't hiring. Get it? I don't know what it's like where you come from, but there's a depression on out here in L.A. and at the same time, all the girls in America have come here to be a star. So it's a little crowded with dolls."

"How much does a girl like me make it pounding the streets? It better be more than picking oranges."

Ramon rubbed his palms together in a businesslike manner. "Well. I won't be paying you, you'll be sharing with me."

"I don't understand."

"You'll be doing a little more than just pitching woo with me. You'll be pitching woo with the world – well, that part of the world that has a little spending money."

"I don't – " She shook her head.

"I'll be your pimp."

"I have no idea what that is."

"I take you to the right part of town and parade you up and down the street. A man will stop his car and ask you how much."

"I won't be some two-bit whore."

Ramon agreed. "Two-bits is fifty cents. I don't know if I can get that much with all the competition around. A two-bit whore was before the depression started. Oh those where the days."

"I know that. It's just an expression left over from when times were better. I mean - I won't be a cheap whore."

"I'll see if I can get about thirty-three cents. Let's see if we can't get that much for you. It ain't sure-fire, though, so don't hold your wig on too tight on my account. And if the war spreads all over and this country is drawn in then we'll make a ton of money. Armies always create entire cities of whorehouses around them where ever they go. Entire cities of nothing but whores! I bet L.A. will have a big Nazi whore camp in one corner, a Jap whore camp in the other, and a Red whore camp in the other – and of course the Yanks get the best one, it being America. Your bonny behind will be in such demand the price might go through the roof! Woo-wee let Hitler and Mussolini bring on the whores! Bring it on! War is good money! "

"How much can I make in a day – even without a war?"

"Slow down." He smiled big. "Maybe I can only get a quarter for you. That's the going rate, but don't worry. There's always some kind of money in pitching woo with the gents, dollface, no matter what, though. Don't worry."

"I worry. I worry. I worry."

"It's Hollywood. The whole town is built on whoppee. The movies are all about whoppee, if you really want to know. So the man in the car pays you a bit of tin. Then you get in the car with him, not afraid of anything, and you'll do what he wants to pop his cork. Or he may even have the time to take you to his room and lay you out for some good ole fashioned missionary work."

"What's that?"

"Missionary position. Like this." She let him push her back on the bed and he lay on top of her. "You get the picture? Good. I better get up now. You're giving me a big long distress signal in my shorts and that always makes me feel like a real punkola. I mean a man." He got up and laughed. She just stared down there, measuring. "But the men in their cars usually don't have time for all that and they just want a quick fat kiss."

"A kiss? Men don't feel satisfied with just a kiss. I know that much."

He undid his belt and some buttons and dropped his pants. "They do if it's right here."

Karin said, "That's disgusting. Who every heard of doing it like that."

Ramon explained, "The doughboys coming home from France after the war picked up some new habits. You know what they say: once they've left the farm and have seen how they do things in Paris – well – there's no going back to the farm. Now are you going to learn this French specialty or am I going to stand here with my pants down whistling Dixie? Now be a doll and go down south on me before the part of me that's still hanging starts to turn blue."

"Learn something French? Sure. I'm certainly never going back to the farm, myself."

"Aaaah!" He pushed her face into himself and while he loudly moaned and made all sorts of other dramatic sounds, she just thought about how he smelled better than her brothers had. She now realized how her being a piece of fun for her brothers had just been a training ground for the game of life. She thought about how she might find a rich producer or director in one of those cars she'd get into. She grew sad, thinking it was probably the most demeaning way of becoming a star, and she wanted to just skip forward to the star part. But life was one moment at a time, and she had to start where she had to start.

She swallowed and asked, unfazed, "I hope everybody doesn't take so long to pop their cork. Do you think I can make a dollar in a day? Silk stockings cost sixty-nine cents. I gotta live!"

He laughed. "Whoa. Hold your horses. You wild woman! I had no idea such a wild woman was hidden behind such a pretty dollface. I've always been warned, behind the prettiest angel faces are the more ferocious she-devils."

"How much money can I make in a day? I gotta know."

Ramon said, "Remember you're sharing with me, sweetheart. I'm your protection, and your man. You have to have somebody to come home to every night so you have a shoulder to cry on."

"How much?"

"Hold your horses. What's your problem? You have a dope problem?"

"I want some Nylon hose."

"I never heard of that. Nylon did you say?"

Karin smiled brightly. "It's keen! Soon everybody will know all about it. And all the stars will wear Nylon. And I'm going to be the biggest star of the 40s. A new great decade, I can just feel it. The depression will go away someday. And if there's a stupid war over there it'll eat itself up. So all that'll be left is America. And we'll be on top of the world. All of us. I'll be the biggest star of America – and that will also make me the biggest star in the world!"

"Well there you go baby, just painting yourself red, white and blue all over. You sure you want to be a star?"

"Sure!"

"Sure?"

"Sure, why not! I'm as good as they are. I've got what it takes."

"Well, baby, you know what they say about talent in this town: there's no shortage of talent - there's just a shortage of talent that can recognize talent."

Karin insisted, "Well I'm going it make it."

"Then I can see I'm not going to have you around forever."

"You kidding? You think I married you? I may be little miss daisy from the sticks, but I know that all you and I can do is use each other as much and as fast as we can before we move on our life along."

Ramon put his palms out again. "Woah, baby, slow down. We just had our first love scene and you're already making me feel old."

"Sorry. I just don't want to ever kid myself. I can't afford it if I'm going to be the biggest Hollywood star ever."

Ramon said, "Well just don't step on my gorgeous mug climbing that ladder to heaven, yet. You know what they say, be nice going up because you'll meet all the same crumbs on the way back down."

Karin scoffed. "Aren't you a pot of happy words. There is no down for me. Only up. I'd kill myself, first."

Ramon said, "Sure, that's what they all say.   But then after they've climbed up to the top of that Hollywoodland sign for the big plunge, then they remember that they'd forgotten that they're suddenly always afraid of heights"

"How do you know so much? How do you know so many things about this town?"

"I tried to be an agent. It's hard. There aren't too many places for an agent when the studios just sign you up outright for your soul for years at a time. And then what is out there is taken up by the William Morris Agency, the hogs. They hog the whole town. But in a year me and my brothers will run this town. We have a plan." He laughed greedily.

Karin nodded. "You and me both. I'd sell my soul if it was for money."

"That don't work around here. The soul only gets about five cents. But they'll pay you fifty dollars for kiss."

"I'd kiss the Three Stooges for a quarter."

Ramon said, "Bet your sweet wallet you would. But don't get ahead of yourself. First you got to make some money the hard way. You got to eat." Ramon patted the bed. "You got to sleep somewhere. And don't forget who your daddy is." He lewdly grabbed himself. "And he ain't a bum steer."

"Yeah, yeah. You'll get your cut, don't worry. And someday when we're old and poisonously rich I'll share some of my champagne with you and we'll laugh our keesters off about this stupid day."

Ramon assured her, "I'll have champagne enough of my own, don't worry. If they still have a France left to make any."

"Where would they all go? Oh I know - into the theater to see me!"

"If a war breaks out in Europe, all those countries over there could just go bye-bye. Who knows? It sounds nasty. It must be hard for you to think so much about the future at a time like this. But then you just stepped off the bus like Shirley Temple."

She slapped his arm. "Oh, you think I'm being corny. But I'm serious. There's all that talk about Germany and Japan. I bet they'll just end up going to war with each other. Then nobody will be left after the war but us over here, because we were smart and stayed out of it. And so then everybody will be looking to Hollywood for stars to love. And so there won't be any French champagne. We'll just drink something else. We'll drink root beer if we have to."

"The way you say that, you remind me of that big movie star, Jeanette MacDonald. She's so sugary that I have to wonder if she's a real musical number in bed, like you."

"Yes, I've been told I look just like her. I just have to fix my eyebrows."

"You'll need lots of makeup – real red rouge for your lips and stuff - and a sparkly dress and then I'll take you to the big whorehouse down Shadow Lane, as they call it, where everybody looks just like a real star up on the screen, and you can be her! They make the top money over there! Two bucks a roll!" His eyes became very wide with greed.

Karin frowned. She wondered how she could become her own star if she was going to be like some other. "And isn't Jeanette about ten years older than I am?"

"That don't matter. They always look eternally young up on the screen. So they won't think you look wrong at all, looking younger.

* * * * *

The next morning after another scrumptious can of corn, Ramon took Karin to a dozen various shops to prove to her that he wasn't lying about how they weren't hiring dolls to smile big behind their notions counters. Two of the clerks were sad for her. Four of them were cold. Six of them laughed in her face. One of them even added, "Working here is just monkey farts. You'd be better off picking oranges."

"I ain't picking no damn oranges." Karin sucked in a deep shaky breath and wiped a tear as she admitted to her new pimp. "Okay. So you're right. You always right?"

Ramon smiled.

"Damn you."

"Hurry up. You walk so slow."

Karin didn't want to. "I'm coming."

They walked past a Warner Brothers movie theater. There were

big posters out front for Confessions of a Nazi Spy starring Edward
G. Robinson. Karin ran inside. "I want to be an usherette! I want
to be an usherette!" Two ushers kicked her out.

They walked past a bald clown holding a shocking bouquet of
dozens of red helium balloons with black swastikas on them. A
placard leaning against a plywood wall read, HEIDENHEIM THE
KLOWN. "You look nice and white," he said to Karin. He gave her
swarthy escort a dirty look. "Take a balloon. Just you. Take one and
then call your congressman and tell him to support Hitler and his
good work. Support Germany. We mustn't let the Fatherland fall to
Jews and perverts."

Karin looked to Ramon. "Should I?"

Ramon just looked at the clown in grave concern and pulled her
along down the street.

"The Jews and the perverts – and the mud people! Don't breed
with the mud people!"

They turned a corner and saw a small parade of people holding
signs that read, White Association of Communists, and WAC They
blandly looked like they all fell out of Central Casting and their
clothes looked like Halloween costume versions of workers. A miner
had black makeup to simulate coal dust on his nose and cheeks. A
butcher had red paint on his paper apron "Workers unite! Workers
unite! But keep all the work for the true Americans who are white!"

The parade turned the corner towards the clown and soon dozens
of red balloons were floating up above a rooftop and into the sky.

Karin said, "Either they scared him or they just killed the damn
clown. A real mob scene. Kicked his head in."

Ramon corrected her. "People just don't kill people – especially
clowns, no matter how scary they get. You got an imagination.
Sheese! Come on."

Karin pointed out, "The communists and the Nazis want to kill
each other."

"Nobody wants to kill anybody. You've read too many magazines.
All people want in life is some honey."

He pointed in the direction of the Hollywoodland sign that was in tiny letters on the very distant hill. "Honey land. Let's try our luck on that next street."

Karin squeezed her own hand tight and told herself not to shake as she skipped to catch up with him and walk alongside. He got to a place he decided he would be happy with He leaned against the large window of a closed shop and she tried to make suggestive poses towards the scant traffic. Soon an old potbellied cop walked by them and warned them, "Keep moving. Make like a bird and scram. If I see you both loitering like this again, I'm booking yah."

Ramon thumbed his nose. "Neeeeeee-yah! Copper, you gotta catch me first!"

The cop sneered right back and fondled his big black pistol, ordering him, "Shake a leg!"

They hurried to a side street. After pausing under a palm tree. Karin nervously pointed. "Look at that. Over there. Tweedle-De-Dum and Twattle-Tee-Twat. The street looks a bit crowded." There were two women under an RC Cola sign and they definitely looked like they were working girls, the way they were dressed up and the way they looked at all the men in the passing cars. They gave Karin and Ramon dirty looks.

"Forget them. They're all wet. You'll get a chance at the traffic, too."

Karin looked at them with jealously. "I think I'll look the part better if I had a louder dress."

"Slow down, doll. You'll have to make some money first. All our first money is going to be poured into making you look like a star so we can make the big bucks down Shadow Lane. You nervous?"

"Yes. What if one of my fans is a murderer?"

"A fan?"

"Sure. If Garbo can call a fan a customer then I can call a customer a fan."

"Sounds sweet to me."

Karin warned him, "And what if he's a murderer out to get me? And good."

Ramon hugged her by one shoulder. "Dollface. Don't blow

your wig over fairy tales. I already told you that people don't really murder other people. It's just stories they make up to sell papers."

"How do I know who's out for me and who's just driving by?"

"Look for the curb crawlers. You can tell. They go too slow and they ain't looking at where they're going. They're looking right at you with a big ole pirate grin on, making glad eyes at you. Then from there on you fly by the seat of your pants."

"They ain't driving around looking for murder?"

He grabbed his pants, to grab at his dick, smiling too big. "Not murder."

Karin asked, "But what if I get an ugly old fat man. A banker! Some pig who eats three times a day!"

"Hold your horses. Just don't start having any kittens. Calm down. Don't be prejudiced. All men need lathered up at least once a day. It's just biology so don't get profound. So you might as well make some money on it. Capitalism. Yankee Doodle Dandy!"

Karin reminded him, "It's illegal."

"Not really. Don't be so off the cob. They don't punish working girls too much and it's hard to prove you were working for it, anyway. Just take what you get, smile at every john like he's special, and if you want to cry about it later on my shoulder, that's why I'm here."

Karin nodded toward the cola sign. "Those girls over there don't look nervous."

"They know what to do. You want a cigarette?"

"I don't smoke."

Ramon lit one for her in his mouth then and stuck it in hers. "You're in Hollywood, now, baby. You need to smoke. It lets the guys driving around looking for you know that you're working. It's an important indicator."

She coughed.

"Slow down. Slow way down. Just make sure you blow a lot of smoke around. People like that. It smells real good. And you'll appreciate the taste of tobacco after you'd had a date who's a real billy goat gruff. A cigarette will cover the taste of anything so you don't flop on your work."

"I'll remember that." She puffed unconvincingly on her cigarette and waved it around like she was a star. "I see it takes some getting used to." She coughed again. "I think I burnt my tongue."

"All good things take some getting used to. And as you get used to it you can breathe it in deeper. Breathe it in as deep as you can. They say it's good for the lungs. It clears out all the mucus. I saw it in an ad the other day in the drug store. Nothing added; it's just a natural ingredient in the tobacco leaf that cleans you out. It's all natural. That makes it good for you. Like tea."

Karin agreed, "And I once read in a magazine how it helps the nerves and digestion. Then I'm glad I'm smoking. A star has to look very healthy. And have healthy nerves."

He added, "All the stars smoke."

Karin asked, "I wonder why? Because it's been proven to be so healthy?"

"And it's important to have smoke catching the movie lights. And when a woman smokes, it makes a man think she's doing that to his dick."

Karin pictured it. "Oh? I never thought of smoking as being suggestive before. And a man smoking? Does a man who smokes really want to be going south on another man?"

"Don't get smart or I'll give you a knuckle sandwich."

Karin replied, "Try and I'll bite your nose off. And then you'll have to go live in the leper colony down in Texas and we'll all be rid of you."

"Hold your horses. Don't get angry. Nobody's been punched, yet. Jeez, I almost believe you."

Karin nodded. "Yep! You ever punch me and I bite your nose off. It's a deal."

"Really?"

She showed him her teeth.

A car stopped in the street. The man in it gave them a mean look.

Ramon pushed her. "Go! Hop in, hurry!"

Karin noticed the two other working girls were laughing at

her. She became even more nervous. She grumbled as she said, "A real sourpuss. Cigarettes better work good." She ran to his open window, winking. "Thirty-three cents, buster. Thirty-five cents and I guarantee you'll be my Old Faithful."

"Send your pimp over here."

"You do mean? Him? I don't think he wants to go south on other men. I don't care what he says about cigarettes."

"No, idiot. I want to speak to your pimp."

Karin waved him over. "Hey!"

Ramon said, "What! You want something special? We're creative, aren't we baby." He said to the man, "You want a three-way? It'll cost you."

He grabbed Ramon's tie and pulled him close. "This is my street, loser. This street is only for my girls." He took out a switchblade and held it to Ramon's neck. "I see you here again – I see you here in five minutes, and I cut you good."

The man put his knife away and drove off.

"Well," Karin said to her red-faced pimp. "That settles it. We aren't staying at this street. You could have been killed."

Ramon scoffed. "He wasn't packing any heat. Just a butter spreader."

"He could have stuck it deep in your neck!"

Ramon laughed nervously. "I said it and it's true. Nobody really murders anybody. If you want cold-blooded murder then buy a trashy dime novel. Those fat cats just act tough like they're real triggermen, but he was a mouse. That's all."

Karin asked, "Oh how do you know he wouldn't murder you? He looked ugly enough about us being here."

"Calm down, dollface. He wouldn't go to prison for life on my account. In real life, people just use guns and knives as a bluff. Believe me."

"Well, the bluff worked for me. Let's get out of here."

They went back to a main street and the potbellied cop was there. He took one look at Ramon and ordered, "Stop!" He blew his whistle. "Stop in the name of the law."

Karin said, "Awe, officer, we're keen. Just walkin'."

"Stop in the name of the law!"

Ramon grabbed Karin's arm. "Run!"

"I can't run."

"Come one!"

Karin was too slow so Ramon started to run away without her.

"Stop or I'll shoot!"

Ramon laughed and kept running, faster.

Karin called out, "Stop!"

"Or I'll shoot!"

Ramon kept running. The cop shot him. The bullet went in the back of his heart, shattered his breastbone and came back out to lodge in a car window. Ramon fell. After a few moments of convulsing and shooting blood across the sidewalk, he was dead.

Karin ran to him. "Oh my God!"

When the cop got there, he decided, "Well, I guess the meat wagon can just take him straight to the morgue."

Karin cried, "You – you – you - didn't have to plug him like that!"

"But I said I would."

"But you know how men are. They get in trouble and they run. They have to. It's just nature. A man can't help it. Running away is natural You can't kill a man for his nature! You didn't have to shoot him for having nature. A man always runs when he's in trouble." She repeated all that a few more times, being so shaken.

The cop frowned down on him. "That's why they gave me a gun. And a bullet. For fools that resist arrest. Now what's your name, little lady? You're going downtown. Now don't you try and give me any trouble. I only had one bullet."

"You don't have anymore bullets?"

"No ma-am, so you'll just have to come peaceably. I ain't gonna be shooting at you today."

Karin jumped up and ran off as she heard swearing yelled very loudly behind her.

She ran through an army of Asian men sweeping the street under a billboard advertising Drums Along The Mohawk starring Henry Fonda and Claudette Colbert. She yelled at Claudette, "You look stupid!" A few of the men looked up at her in her white doily cap.

When Karin passed a hardware store, she went in and asked, "Please, do you have a job. I'll do anything. I'll sweep the floor."

"Do you see a help wanted sign out front? No."

Karin tried not to look too desperate. "Oh please."

The clerk frowned. "I have to feel sad for someone who looks so desperate. I have a brother who works picking grapes north of here. He says jobs open up now and again. And you can pop a grape in your mouth every now and again so you don't drop dead."

Karin lifted her chin. "Oh, that's right. I'm going to be a star." She left.

The clerk shook his head. "You'll have to find your marbles first."

Chapter Three

A few hours later when she got to the door of the converted carriage house, she realized she didn't have a key. She collapsed on the doorstep and bawled.

A Mexican woman with a mop bucket walked by and looked at her funny. "Your poor peepers."

Karin wiped her tears and said, "I locked myself out. Um - my husband will be out all day and I forgot the key - and I have to use the toilet."

"I have a passkey. If you lock yourself out, just go to the main house and you can walk right in, underground."

"What?"

"There's a hallway underground from the main house to here, with the coal furnace in-between. You just go right past the old kitchen and you can't miss it. There's no toilet back here, anyway. The only toilet is in the main house."

"Oh. I didn't know that." She felt exposed. "That sounds ducky."

"Well now you know everything." The Mexican woman let her in with her big long iron passkey.

Karin hoped her stupid pimp had left some cash in the room. She looked everywhere. She only found a few more cans of food, a cheap shaving kit and an extra pair of boxer shorts. No glorious rolls of cash – not even in the pillows or mattress. "Damn! Why didn't I pick his pockets after he'd been shot?"

She lay on the bed and thought about how she didn't know anything about Ramon. It left her feeling strangely empty. The feeling was so horrible that she was sure the room would collapse and smash her into the ground. She wanted to get drunk. After spending the night, she ate all the cans of food and then snuck away. Without a hundred dollar movie star dress she went, anyway, to Shadow Lane.

A woman who looked like she thought she looked like Bette Davis answered the door with great suspicion. "If you're from the Salvation Army, go away. I hate the bugle. Do you know what time of day it is? We're all hung-over!"

Karin smiled. "They say I look just like Jeanette MacDonald."

The Bette Davis opened the door wider, getting her drift. "Oh? Well we already have three Jeanette MacDonalds."

Karin was surprised. "You do? Men like wholesome women that much?"

A middle-aged dwarf in child's pajamas and fat blonde curls under a hood that had bunny ears walked up to them and asked. "Where do you keep the aspirin?"

The Bette Davis replied, angrily. "I just gave you two aspirin."

"I just puked."

"Hold on!" The Bette Davis yelled and then returned to Karin. "As you can see, the cathouse is busy. And we don't need your mug. Now if we could just get a Shirley Temple that doesn't puke so much."

The Shirley Temple asked Karin, "Do you know how to get rid of wrinkles? I gotta get rid of my wrinkles."

"Please! I'm desperate! Then hire me as Karin Panotchitch!"

"Who's she?"

Karin tried not to cry. "She's real kippy! She's me! And I'm going to be a star! And you'll have the real thing! Even before it happens!"

The Bette Davis frowned. "You poor doll. You're really beat, aren't you. This town is full of seals without any tricks. So you get a sardine for trying." She fished into a pocket in the sleeve of her yellow silk kimono and held out a little dried brown thing. "A dizzy mushroom, actually."

"Dizzy?"

"It's all yours for being the sorriest thing to come to my door since – since - since that sixty year old thing that thought she was Mae West. Oh my god! As if such a star would ever let herself be sixty. She had a turkey wobble! Christ! And she thought she was walking like Mae West. Glory! She only looked like a six story hotel during the San Francisco earthquake." The Bette Davis did a jerking halting hula-hoop impersonation and then laughed cruelly.

Karin looked at the little brown thing in her palm. "Dizzy? Mushroom? What?"

"You ever had a dizzy mushroom?"

Karin shook her head. "Oh course not. There's no such thing."

The Bette Davis laughed. "Just try it and see. And never come back unless all of our other Jeanette MacDonald's drop dead. Oh, come to think of it, I heard that a lousy slut from The Gold Rush shot up too much dope and dropped dead. Go there."

"The Gold Rush?"

"Maybe Mama Gravy will take you on over there. She don't do movie stars so she don't pay good. But that's all I can say." The Bette Davis slammed the door angrily.

Karin looked at her scrap of dizzy mushroom in confusion. She wondered what it meant. She ate it mostly because she was in the mood for a snack. It didn't make much of one. Then she felt herself get some energy. The sun got brighter and she could see around and through corners. She ran to them and was in a studio back lot. She ran into the doors of Notre Dame and came out on a western street. A few gargoyles from the cathedral were lying around on their sides amongst discarded RC Cola bottles. Several Look Magazine pages blew by. She ran down the street and came to a painted backdrop of an ocean liner. In front of it was a car full of bullet holes and a large sphinx with some of its surface peeling off to show chicken wire. She ran to another street and was in Merry Old England but a whole collection of Greek temple pillars were also stashed there, along with a few stuffed canvas dress dummies and sculptures of cacti carved out of cork. She had to climb through the black metal skeleton of a zeppelin to get out the other side, to a crossroads with New York one way and the Congo, the other. Straight ahead, past a few sand dunes from a patch of desert was a tall pile several stories high made up of bits and piece of all sorts of things, and a crane was dropping a castle tower onto it. It flattened with a violent crunch as it landed. A few ballroom star chandeliers fell. Then the crane dropped Cinderella's coach. It splattered open when it hit, tearing in a way to show it had been made of brittle paper and plaster. Some glitter lazily followed, brightly catching the sun. Karin loudly gasped as she realized she was at a dream dump. After the crane went way, she crossed the patch of desert, hearing thin wooden boards under the sand dunes creak under her slight weight. She climbed up into the pile but fell often into it, sinking into paper boulders, cardboard tree trunks, dungeon walls painted on framed canvas, and other things that weren't as solid as they'd looked from even a few yards away. Finally, thanks to the sturdy legs of a wooden giraffe and a trellis of blue silk flowers, she got to the very top. Holding onto the torch for balance, she stood on the green arm of a diminutive Statue of Liberty. From her great lofty view, she couldn't see anything. She was in a black impenetrable vortex. Then she heard a loud rip and fell through the sails of a clipper ship, through a painting of Claudette Colbert's forehead, and went deep into the center of the dream dump. She tore at dark crystal cave made of wiggly cellophane, climbed though the cockpit of an airplane, parted the drooping tentacles of a rubber octopus, and ended up crawling towards a bright light until she squeezed out of the mouth of a giant poodle and was on her hands and knees at the desert again. She looked back in amusement and realized she'd just been born out of a poodle. She laughed. She laughed herself delirious. A clown, a cowboy and a pirate heard her and came by and carried her away. They passed a harem of tall men who were dressed up like belly dancers. She could see the shadows of their swaying genitals through their gossamer skirts and she laughed even harder. A giant five story jerky gorilla was trying not to fall down. A Salvation Army bugle played taps just for her. She was tossed in a ditch behind a dusty row of shops.

Karin woke up in ditch and a foot long lizard was looking at her. He puffed out his neck angrily. It repulsed her and she thought of throwing a rock at it, but instead she just grumbled at it. "Okay. It's your ditch. I'm scramming."

She walked dizzily behind a row of dusty shops and wondered

if she'd just dreamed that she'd been on a studio back lot, or if she really had, somehow. It had seemed so real. It seemed more real than anything else she'd ever seen in her whole life. She decided that she was too dizzy to walk around. With great effort she made her way back to the ditch, and ignoring the territorial ballooning lizard, fell down in it again and started to snore.

At sunrise, Karin walked down a few streets and then leaned against a palm tree. She looked up into its browning leaves and said, "I hate everything. I hate everybody. I even hate you. I hate the trees. They get to just live by taking in the sun. I hate the trees!"

A man, passing, tipped his black derby hat at her. "Hey droopy drawers, don't you sound all wet."

"A star shouldn't sound all wet. Should she." Karin forced herself to smile. "I'm going to be a star. I was even on a studio back lot. And it wasn't a tour. I had the whole place to myself."

"You look rather droopy drawers this morning. You'd think you'd been sent over by Central Casting to play a part in The Grapes of Wrath."

Karin looked around. "What's that?"

He suddenly acted all smart. "Oh, I read they're going to make it into a movie and plan on having it out sometime next year. Maybe they'll need a lot of extras."

"No. I mean, what's Central Casting?"

"You don't know? We all go there to get work in the movies. I've been in six. As an extra. I've been to all the different studios to help fill up their different scenes. Once I even got close enough to say hi to Errol Flynn when we were all dressed up funny for Robin Hood That was my best part. Usually you just wear your own clothes but that time they gave me something made special just for me, and told me I looked good in tights. Nice knees, they said."

"How was Errol Flynn?"

"He was aces!"

Karin became filled with great hope. "Really? Central Casting can make you a star?"

"A star?"

"I'm going to be a star. I big hit. A success."

"Most stars burn out in a flash." He pointed to a distant billboard advertising Beau Geste. "How long do you think even a Gary Cooper can last?"

Karin said, "I don't care. I want my chance."

"You don't want to be an actor. They're the lowest. They say of an actor's shelf life – that even if he gets success, it's only delayed failure."

Karin waved him off. "That's malarkey. You got to try. You got to try as hard as you can!"

"Well, sorry kid, they don't make stars at Central Casting. No, they just fill up the backgrounds with faces."

Karin took a step back. "Well, then, awe, how do you become a star?"

"I'd say make it in New York, first. Be a star there so they send for you. That's how you get this town to treat you with any respect. If you want to be a star, at all in your condition, work at The Gold Rush." He chuckled lewdly.

"What's that? I heard about that place before. What do you know about it?"

"That's a place where a man finds a lot of nice dancehall hostesses."

"Oh?" Karin's mind reeled. "And producers and directors go to this place?"

"Maybe. Why not? They go anyplace, I suppose. You a working girl?"

"Maybe. I got to eat, too."

"You don't mind if people use you like that?"

"Not if I can use them right back. Whoever said life was fair? I heard what they say about the casting couch. I have nothing against any couch. Don't knock it. It's better than the floor."

"You want to come back with me to my car."

"For what?"

"A picnic."

"What kind?"

"My kind."

He unbuttoned his fly and left it that way. "I know a nice little alley. There's a locked gate so nobody will bother us."

Karin asked, "How you going to get in if it's locked?"

"I open it from the other side. The hinges are loose. If it didn't stay locked, it'd fall off."

Karin said, "Sure, okay. It'll set you back a quarter."

He nodded knowingly. "I know the score."

"I hope your car isn't far."

"It's down the block. You stay there. I'll come pick you up."

"Give me your tin first. Then I'll be waiting for you like a good girl."

"What if you run? What if you try and chisel me?"

Karin smiled wickedly. "Then run me over."

He smiled like it might be fun. "Here." He gave her some coins. "I like your style. You stay right there, dollface, and I'll be back in a heartbeat. I feel my heartbeat already, and it ain't beating anywhere near my heart anymore. Oh glory!"

"And give me a cigarette."

He lit one up for her," and repeated, "In a heartbeat." He fluttered his hands over his heart for a moment like he was going to sing an Al Jolson song, and then ran off.

As she blew smoke all around like she was something important, all Karin could think was, "Men." She didn't know whether to laugh or scream.

She saw his car coming. She saw the giant smile on his face. She saw that he didn't look for traffic at the cross street. She saw a truck plow into his side of his car. He pounded down sideways onto his seat, bounced back up like on a trampoline, and then fell back down. When he bounced back up again, she could see he was knocked out. When he fell down out of sight for a final time, she frowned and walked away. She wondered if she was cursed.

* * * * *

She went to a telephone directory to try and find out where The Gold Rush dancehall was. It wasn't listed, but while looking at all the names, she realized her name wasn't very movie star sounding, and the K was too German looking. Germany wasn't very popular these days. She would be popular. The first thing that came to her mind, as a better Englishy sounding choice from Karin, was Carol. And if she chopped off most of her awkward last name, Panotchitch, she was Carol Pan.

"Carol Pan! Golly! I like that. That's snazzy! From now on, I'm Carol Pan. We are going to be a star!"

She asked around about the dance hall until a man gave her directions. She hopped on a streetcar. A nun in glowing white robes sat next to her. Carol said, " I wouldn't want your laundry bill. You look so clean."

The nun smiled. "Yes. Clean. Inside and out."

Carol asked, "What kind of nun are you? A very powerful nun?"

"I'm a Franciscan."

Carol still marveled. "Nuns always wear white, don't they? Your white is so white."

"Franciscan nuns usually wear brown. But I wear white. Because I am Sister Agatha of the Streetcar."

Carol asked, "Do you pray to bones?"

"No. I pray to the Mother of God."

Carol thought about that a moment and said, "I wonder if I can pray to my mother."

The nun said knowingly, "She's dead."

Carol grew sad at the memory. "She got gored by a bull. And then after that, Father didn't care about us kids and tried to kill himself and leave us all abandoned. But he failed and so he got rid of all the cattle and we went into sheep. But he got killed later anyway. A tractor ran over his head and it wasn't even his own tractor."

The nun asked, "You miss your Mother terribly?"

Carol thought about that. "I don't know. It was so long ago. We used to cook together. I was the only daughter. I have six brothers."

The nun looked sadly upon Carol. "And they didn't help you out. Did they. In fact they helped dirty your soul."

"I don't want to talk about them."

The nun smiled. "I'm Sister Agatha of the Streetcar. I'm glad to be your friend."

"Of the - streetcar? Isn't that odd?"

The nun regarded the other passengers. "This is my mission. The streetcar is where many lost souls find themselves. Going somewhere. Going nowhere. To the ocean. To the canyons. To the hills. To the movies. To their jobs. Going nowhere."

Carol asked, "And what are you going to tell me to help my soul?"

The nun did some bad acting to pretend she was thinking, before she said, "I'm going to say a prayer about the Mother of God. You need a mother."

Carol agreed, "Yes, sometimes I feel like I need a mother so badly I could just stop breathing. Like my head is underwater. And it's hot water. Hot water full of dead fish and they're all smashed against my cheeks. You ever feel that way?"

The nun closed her eyes and softly prayed, "Remember, most loving Virgin Mary, never was it heard that anyone who turned to you for help was left unaided. Inspired by this confidence, though burdened by my sins, I run to your protection for you are my mother. Mother of the Word of God, do not despise my words of pleading but be merciful and hear my prayer. Amen."

Carol was dissolving in tears. "I gotta go!" She ran off.

* * * * *

Carol walked past a white wall that had graffiti painted on it in red letters, Hollywood and Gomorrah. Repent today or the whole town burns She tried to remember exactly what had happened in the Bible story and wondered if that was the one where everyone fell off the tower of Babylon and learned English. Or forgot English. Or learned French. Or learned French ways of making a bit of dough by going south on a gent so you wouldn't get a baby in the oven out of it. And then a city or two all burned down, turning some lady into a pillar of salt. Carol was confused at how that all fit together.

"I'll ask the nun next time I see her. Or maybe not. I wouldn't want to embarrass her; I think it's a naughty story."

Carol saw an uneven hand-painted sign, The Gold Rush. She went down a lane of bushes that badly needed cut back. The tips of their branches scratched at her arms and stirred up a few winged bugs. She nervously pushed through thin wood doors. Sagging paper decorations hung from the ceiling from some year when there was an extra sixty cents to blow. They looked so sad that they reminded her of her visit to the dream dump. She shivered.

"Hello?" Carol called out, feeling small.

"What!" A voice came from the corner of the dance floor. Mama Gravy, a woman in her thirties with her hair cut in a severe and dated red bob, as if her heyday was the roaring twenties and she was stuck there, looked at her from where she was lounging in a canvas chair. "My aren't you pretty. Good. We just lost a good slut to dope. You dance? You do all the rest?" Mama Gravy carefully put her hand-rolled cigarette out on the arm of her chair so that she could light it back up again later.

Carol said, "Sure. You have a place for me?"

Mama Gravy got up with an irritated groan. "Maybe. Sure. Depends.   You and your giddy aunt."

Carol was confused. She put her chin out. "Yes or no."

Mama Gravy covered her mouth and hacked the last of the smoke from her lungs. Then she looked closely at her palm. "Good. No blood yet. All the Okies are bringing TB into town. I bet it's them. It's such a dirty place over there with all that dust. They don't call it the dirty thirties for nothing."

"Sure."

Mama Gravy regarded Carol. "Hmmm. You might make a dance hall hostess. Maybe. If you can really dance and show some guts. You're pretty enough. A real tomato. And my, are you not a picture of youth - a sweet thing a girl only has once." She put out her hand. "Slip me a five. I'm Mama Gravy. I own the hall so you're talking to the right person. And you're hired if you can dance. And all the rest. Just expect to make more calluses than dollars."

"On my feet?"

"Yeah, there too. What's your name?"

"I'm Kar- I mean, Carol! Carol Pan!"

Mama Gravy gestured for her to turn. "So thin. You need to either fatten up or fall down."

Carol smiled. "It's picture weight, they say. I look like I'm ready to be a star."

Mama Gravy laughed. "You have a better chance in this town of getting hit by lightening. You have a better chance of getting hit by lightening every Wednesday for the full month of December."

"I'll do my best."

Mama Gravy held out her arms. "Dance with me and I'll be able to tell you if you have a job. It's an audition. If you can dance with me, you can dance with anybody. I got two meat hooks and a mind like any fellah."

"Sure."

Mama Gravy took Carol in her arms and then squeezed her tight into her bosom. "Swell. You a cement mixer?"

"What's that?"

"A bad dancer."

Carol said, "I think I dance okay."

"Just keep off my feet. That's all I care about. Ooooh, and you got a pretty toosh back there." She grabbed Carol's rump and felt it up.

"It's okay."

"No. Not much meat back there. But nice enough."

Carol wished the woman would stop feeling her like that. So she finally said, nervously, "Do you get many movie producers and directors in here?"

Mama Gravy felt Carol's bosom. "A bit anemic in this department, too. Some men like to have something smashed into their tie when they dance. If they want to dance with something as flat as you then they can join the army. In fact, once we had an old army colonel who had a bigger bust size than you. Much."

"Ouch! You're going to turn my nipples into applesauce. You get many movie producers and directors in here?"

"No - not too many film folk. Not from the big studios anyway. They're in their own bubble. A very golden bubble. But that bubble is overdue for popping. They've just used up all their gas, gone bankrupt and they're pretty scared behind those big tall studio walls - like they're held up in castles waiting to pour hot oil on us if we don't go to their stupid movies. Boy, are the pictures getting bad. They just don't make 'em like they used to."

Carol was alarmed. "Really?"

Mama Gravy looked off in thought. "I don't know, I just think Hollywood is slipping really bad - running out of steam. Have you heard about the line-up of new films coming out this year? Pathetic. 1939 will be this town's final joke before it finally falls on its face for good and proves what they've been saying all decade long."

"What."

"Capitalism is dying fast and for good. So whoop it up and buy all them jewels and pearls and shoes and cars and caviar and fine things now while you can." She laughed.

Carol said, "I read that Joan Crawford is a good skate. She ice-skates in her new picture. Everybody does. They just put everything on ice. That sounds keen to me."

"That's just what I'm talking about. On ice. See? They've run out of things to make movies about. Did you hear about that Gone With The Wind they're making?"

Carol nodded. "Sure. Everybody has."

"Everybody's drumming up the movie with such desperation it only makes me suspicious. I bet the film is really a stinker and will only last a week at the theaters and then disappear, once the public sees what it really is. Clark Gable didn't want to be in it. He did everything he could to get out of it. That tells me something."

Carol said, "I'm sure MGM will do a beautiful job. They always do. They're pretty kippy.   And Gable was just bellyaching. They always twist people's arms to be in things. I don't know why. You'd think the stars would be grateful for parts. I'd take a part real fast."

"Fiddle-dee-dee. At MGM they make everything so glittery and pious.   Only at MGM could that sugary Jeanette MacDonald sing pretty high notes after a big earthquake."

"They say I look like her."

Mama Gravy said, "Pray you don't. People will start kneeling at you in prayer like Clark Gable - and wanting high notes after their house has fallen down. Horrors."

"Didn't that movie do well?"

"The whole town falls down and she's singing like she's in a choir loft. It's all wet. She's all yesterday's news by now and she'll be forgotten for all time."

Karin said, "But Gone With the Wind is all the talk right now."

Mama Gravy held Carol even closer and swayed her hips lewdly. "That's just hype you hear. That's just the studio putting itself in print so it can read all about itself. MGM is good at blowing hot air for itself. Believe me. They have public mind control and mass hypnosis down, I'm sure. But that's not my point. Who wants a war picture right now? Hitler is making trouble in Europe and people have been saying he's going to start a war and I say that nobody wants to think about war right now. Right now war is a nightmare that's just too close for comfort for anybody. Nobody will come close to the movie theater, come the day it opens. Especially in the South. Some Yankees up North will show up to gloat, I suppose. But most other people will find such a topic distasteful in these times. Mark my words. And also mark my words. That other big expensive MGM production will flop and be gone in a week and never heard from again. The Wizard of Oz. Have you read the original books?"

Karin shook her head. "But I heard about it. It's a fantasy. Right? There were silver shoes and a yellow brick road going to places."

"I saw pictures of it in a magazine and I got so mad. Damn I got mad!" She grabbed Carol's behind, again, and pulled her tight. "They

modernized it all. It's all art deco! It doesn't have the charming
look of the original illustrations at all that I loved so much when
I was a little girl! And they say the lion and tin man and scarecrow
are playing it like big loud vaudeville hams. That sounds so wrong.
What does a bunch of old hammy Berlin Jews have to do with a
fantasy place called Oz? I can't imagine it working at all. And Judy
Garland is just too old to play the part of Dorothy. She's supposed
to be a little girl. Judy has all grown up. A girl that old, playing that
part, is embarrassing for her."

Carol just nodded. She was old enough to starve in the streets
but yet was a year younger than the actress that would play a little girl
living with her Auntie Em.

Mama Gravy continued, "And Judy's so modern – so swing. I
just can't see it. I have nothing against Judy. I saw her past picture,
Love Finds Andy Hardy, and it was a hoot. They all talked about
how Lana Turner was the looker but Judy stole the show. But that
was that kind of show."

"Yeah, you can't have romance on the yellow brick road."

Mama Gravy sadly moaned. "I loved the books so much when
I was little. I know it's probably hard to do fantasy in the movies
and get it all to come together, but you'd think MGM was trying to
make it a big loud ugly mess just on purpose to remind us again how
it knows how. I bet there won't be a single moment where it feels
magic. You'll just see hammy old stars in front of art deco sets and
then you'll run home crying to your books."

Carol said, "Something has to come out this year that'll be
good."

Mama Gravy grabbed the back of Carol's hair to put her head on
her shoulder. "And that Joan Crawford is back again later this year
with The Woman. MGM again. So you know they'll just ruin that
play. And mark my words, after this movie, you'll never hear from
Joan Crawford again. She's all used up. She's old. She did silent
films. She had the 30s and now new fresh stars will take over. That
Joan Crawford hasn't had a real hit in a while and she's just run out
of chances. I read that this time she plays a bitch. So she's through

for good. She's spit in the face of those fans she has left. Nobody wants to see a Joan Crawford type play a bitch. Absurd. Who could imagine such a sad thing? MGM has done it again. Strike three and MGM is out. I don't have a crystal ball, but I can just tell those three boondoggles will be the flops that take MGM down. And down hard."

Carol said, "Well, there has to be some other studios this year that'll make something good, that people will want to see."

Mama Gravy decreed, "And you'll never hear the name John Wayne again."

"Who's he? That cowboy?"

"He just did lots of B movies - westerns for Republic and Monogram. Now he's in a big expensive movie coming out for United Artists called Stagecoach. That'll be a big fat boring flop. I saw a picture from it in the magazine and who wants to watch people sitting in a cramped stagecoach for hours all talking to each other in some serious movie from United Artists. Now if Republic was doing it, it'd a smash. The stagecoaches in their pictures always go a hundred miles an hour, Get shot up with bullets and arrows and cannons, get hit by flash floods, cyclones and earthquakes, roll off cliffs into the sea, and are all ablaze and roll a few times. And that's at least in the first ten minutes. At least." She took her head off Carol's shoulder and winked in her face. "Republic knows how to make excitement the big studios just don't understand. The majors are more worried about if a star is anywhere nearby and how to light her pretty little face so that she glows like a goddam chandelier." She kissed Carol.

Carol felt very stupid so she broke the kiss by saying, "They do all the serials, don't they? At Republic? The Lone Ranger?"

"Mark my words. The thirties are over. And with it will go Joan Wayne, poor fellah. Nobody will ever hear from him again after this pretentious high hat flop. Everything United Artists does is high flatulent and pretentious. John Wayne won't get another chance at an A picture. That's just how it works."

"Maybe the Indians will attack and make it exciting."

"Well, as I said, I think people will shy away from war pictures for a long while to come now, due to that Hitler and what a crumb he is. We just don't want to go to the movies and be reminded of that kind of thing these days. It's just too horrible to joke about and make money on. I just hope it puts everybody in the mood to go to the whorehouse."

Carol agreed. "Yes, everything I've heard about what's going on overseas does sound all wet. But that's far away and will never bother us. I'm sure. Hitler is a crumb."

"I hope you're right. And I bet you'll never hear from Bette Davis again, after the thirties have passed. She's just a relic of a Hollywood that was. Now we'll get new stars. Every decade you get new stars."

"Like me."

Mama Gravy said, "Don't get too fancy." Mama Gravy moved in for another kiss.

So Carol said, "Boy, you can see through a brick wall better than most. What stars do you think will make it big, that are just starting out right now?"

"Watch for Priscilla Lane. She was so exciting in The Roaring Twenties I peed a roaring flower garden all over my theater seat. She was such a tomato! I can just feel they'll trade in all the old stars for new ones, like cars. It happened at the end of the twenties. And watch Francis Farmer. She's new and will be at the very top of the heap in a year or two. She so beautiful and she's got real talent – a real spark that makes you want to look at her. When I saw her in Ride a Crooked Mile I just had to hang on tight to myself, and I don't mean to my other hand."

"Yes, she's such a beautiful star."

"Francis will keep rising if Hollywood survives, and she'll end up being the biggest star of the 40s, mark my word. But the industry will flop in a big way from what's coming out this year, and I hope it can bounce back. But for all of next year, and a long time to come, I bet the stinkers coming out will sink the whole town into bankruptcy, completely. Hollywood has escaped the effects of the Great Depression for a while. It's time they paid. It's time they went bankrupt like everybody else."

Carol asked, "But - but then how will I become a star?"

"My advice is to go to one of the B studios, like Republic. They haven't spent all their money on a few foolish overweight films on unpopular topics. They spend so little that they can't flop. Republic spends on one picture, to make the whole picture, what MGM spends just on catering. And in the B movies there's a lot of chases - and things blow up. And there's lots of shooting. People like that. So when United Artists and Paramount and MGM all go under, it's the B studios that'll rise and take their place. That's my prediction for how 1939 will go out. After the flop of The Wizard of Oz embarrasses Judy Garland off the screen. And then she'll be forgotten for all time. For a child star, it'll be Shirley Temple that will be the one remembered. Mark my words. It's hard for a child star to grow up."

"Poor Judy. It's hard to be a child star and then grow old. How sad she had to do The Wizard of Oz. How sad for her."

Mama Gravy nodded. "Yes, it's sad but it's a cruel town. And Marlene Dietrich too. She'll be forgotten for all time. She'll be through after her western flops. What's miss fancy pants doing in a western? She's not a western star. She'll be snored off the screen. Destry Rides Again won't save her from being box office poison. They'll just burn all the prints, I bet, and it'll be forgotten for all time. She'll run back to Germany with her tail between her legs. Mark my words. And Paramount, her studio, didn't even make Destry. They were through with her since she's lost them so much money these last few years. Universal made it. Boy will Universal be smarting after their Marlene Dietrich western fails. Yep, I'm right, now that I think about it. Only the B studios like Republic will survive into the 40s. Someday, people will have no idea what MGM even was. Oh listen to me. I'm talking too much. Must have been that reefer."

"You smoked a reefer?"

"Yeah. When you was coming in. My nerves."

Carol had wondered why the woman had smelled like a burnt hay bale that had some stinkweed caught up in it. "Oh."

Mama Gravy misinterpreted her expression. "And you may think I'm taking my meat hooks at you like a caveman, well sugar pie, just wait until the real gents have at you. Most gents just like to get at least one good pinch in. A good hard one. They're not happy until they've seen you react to them hurting you. They want to put a little bruise mark on you as if that somehow makes you theirs. Like a dog peeing on a tree. Don't be proud when you get pinched. Cry out good and loud. It'll make the gent happy and he'll have gotten that out of his system and won't want to pinch you again. I don't know why most men like to see hurt like that. It must be a caveman sort of leftover."

"I can't wait."

"Yeah, I been talking too much. And maybe it's just your sweet face. A person can get themselves in trouble talking to a person too much. Even a person like you. You look so sweet and so they spill their guts and say way too much." Mama Gravy let go of Carol's hips, backed away and sized her up. "I hope you have a dress other than that one. It looks more flea bitten than my piano player, and almost smells worse than his feet."

"No. What you see is all I own in the whole world."

"You poor dear. No wonder you're trying so hard to dance better than you dance. The depression left you good and beat, did it. I'll take you on and you can have some dresses left behind if you work it off. It's ten dollars worth. Maybe more. A good day dress is three dollars these days. And there's at least four of them. Come in the back and I'll show you." They went into a narrow dark hall and stepped down two uneven steps into a small but long room. Bunk beds were on one side. "You sleep here. All twelve of you."

"One, two, three, four, five, six, seven, eight. I only count eight beds."

Mama Gravy said dispassionately, "I hope you don't mind bumping pussy."

"What? What's that?"

"You double up, muffin. This isn't the Ritz. We usually get a two dog night, no matter what the day was like, anyway, so you won't complain."

Carol didn't know the expression. "Two dog night?"

"It's what the natives say. If it takes two dogs to sleep with to keep you warm, then it's a two dog night. Sometimes it's a three dog night and the desert feels like ice. Cold cold cold. I don't know. It's just an expression."

"Oh. Sure."

Mama Gravy opened a wardrobe and took out a few dresses and held them up to Carol. "The old doll that dropped dead was a bit taller than you but it's okay if these things hang a little long. You'll look just doggy – but that's better then what you look like now. A nothing."

"She died?"

"She did too much morphine. She said it took away the pain. Then she came back from a wedding in her family and that's what really finally did her in. So she can say her bride sister killed her. Shame. She'd just bought the most hideous dress for the occasion. She was a bride's maid. I always thought I wanted to be somebody's bride's maid someday until I saw this dress." Mama Gravy took it out. "I'll throw it in for no extra cost, just as long as you don't dance in it."

Carol touched the fabric, expecting it to shatter. "What is it?"

"Some sort of crepe, they say, but I didn't know crepe was supposed to look so much like dead corn husk. They must have made this in Oklahoma - dead crops is all they know. And the way there's so much of it bunched up in the back, I'd be afraid of termites. A squirrel could live back here and you'd never know for a week. What a shame to hide the ass."

Carol sighed, wishing it was anything like what the stars wore. "It's a dress."

"Wear these other ones when you dance. You can't wear this awful crepe. I think these skirts would be far too long on you, anyway. Unless you don't mind just being dragged around the dance floor, sideways."

"What?"

"Just kidding. Keep on your feet or you're sacked."

"Of course."

"Come this way. Now I'll show you the nice bedroom a gent takes you to if he wants to pull out his giggle stick and drill for gold. The room is called Sutter's Mill."

Carol regarded the bed and her stomach soured. "Oh. That's why you call this place the Gold Rush."

"Yep. Drill for fool's gold and we hope they rush. There's nothing worse than a fairy who comes in wondering if he can prove his masculinity and he can't. A half hour later we just pull him off and tell him to scram. Or sometimes they just come in too drunk. That's usually the case. A hootched up man is truly a wet sock. He's so randy but can't do anything about it. Nothing but give you a pinch."

"Sure."

"I mean it. Drunk men are the worse. Didn't Shakespeare say something about it once?"

Carol admitted, "I wouldn't know a lick of that."

"Well he said something about having all desire but no means. Ha ha."

"Sure."

Mama Gravy pointed to a door. "And here's where you girls get to wash up. I tell you what. You wash up right now and slip into one of these dresses."

"Thanks." In a closet was a shower. The ceiling had a hole for natural light to shine in. Carol said to her new boss, "Bye-bye."

"No. I'm staying right here. I'll just watch to make sure you don't use up all my water."

"I shower alone. Bye-bye."

"I'm the boss. I can watch what I want."

Carol stated, "You want to watch me shower? Give me a quarter."

"I like your style. I've met a lot of hardboiled eggs but you're twenty minutes. And as for water, you only get three minutes of water so make sure all the soap is off or you're stuck wearing it for a long while." Mama Gravy slammed the door, and hard.

Chapter Four

That evening, just before the dance hall opened, Mama Gravy took Carol to the floor for further instruction. Carol asked, "And dance with me nicer this time."

"The men won't. But some of them are shy. You need to help remind them of what's in their own wear-abouts."

"Whereabouts?"

Mama Gravy explained, "Shorts. Tell a dirty joke, otherwise it ain't to the backroom to make hay - to make that extra quarter. Some men just start to dance and think you're a lady and they get all mannered and proper."

Carol said, "But I am a lady, right?"

"You may act all high and removed, and that's fine. But by definition, a lady is a woman who don't have to work for living. She don't break a sweat. If she's a real lady then her husband don't even have to work for a living, either. She don't even lift a finger to raise her own children. The help does that. The help in the name of the nanny. A lady can be very busy, though. Her long day is crowded with social obligations and very private ones, too. She has luncheons for important gossip, and numerous charity events to attend or organize all by herself, tombolas and hospital visits with baskets of fruit, and she works behind the scenes in all levels of politics in great stealth to give the illusion that it's really a man's world and she didn't do a thing. Ah. I'd love to be a real lady. It sounds so fulfilling."

Carol asked, "If a lady is all that, then what's a working girl called?"

Mama Gravy was confounded. "Hmm. Well - she was called a wench. But that word has fallen out of use completely in our modern times. It's become a bad word. That's odd."

"What?"

"It's odd how words about people who have to work for a living have become the bad words. We look down on working people even

though we all have to work. Like the word villain. That one, too.
That word used to just mean farmhand Now why would a farmhand
turn into a bad word? It comes from the word villa – a servant at the
villa.   It just goes to show you - the ones who work the hardest get
thought of with disgust. What do we call a working girl today? I
really don't know. Oh wait. I know now, we call her a working girl.
That's it."

"You sure know lots about words."

Mama Gravy smiled proudly. "I was once going to be a school
teacher. I went to college for it for one whole year. In fact, I
was thinking for a time to be a nun and teach at a nice Catholic
school."

"You? A nun?" Carol laughed.

"Don't laugh. That was a long time ago. I was young and full of
big ideals. I even believed in religion. Me."

"You don't believe in Jesus now?"

Mama Gravy replied, "Sure. Just like I'm sure Paul Bunyan was
once a real person."

Carol pointed out, "But Paul Bunyan ain't a religion."

Mama Gravy belted out a laugh. "Thank God or we'd all be
afraid to go into the woods."

"What happened? Why did you quit college? The real reason."

Mama Gravy explained, "We finally went out to some schools
one day and we talked to the children. To real live children. And I
realized something rather basic about myself that disqualified myself.
I hate children."

"What?"

"I'd only been around students my own age, before then. Then
I found out I hated children. They are so – so – tiny and soft and
– and - stupid. I can't stop thinking out how they're all so – so – so
- " She shuddered. "And their awful little voices!"

Carol nodded. "Oh, yes. You have to be around children if you
teach school."

Mama Gravy smiled at her memory. "I did love the company of
the other teachers. Those were the finest women I've ever known."

The she frowned at a memory.

Carol asked, "Then why is your name Mama?"

"It has nothing to do with children."

"Then what?"

Mama Gravy grew irritated. "You're too nosey. You're bringing back some terrible memories." She sighed like her heart had broken.

Carol worked hard to remember the original point of their conversation. "Oh! And how do we get shy men to remember what's in their own drawers?"

"Oh that. I always find that a dirty joke helps. And it helps even more if you can personalize it some."

Carol lied, "I don't know any dirty jokes."

"Oh sure, "Mama Gravy said with a lewd wink. "Here's one that helps. A man walks into a clock shop and walks up to the counter and unbuttons his pants and takes out his giggle stick and puts it on the counter and the shop girl says, What did you do that for? And the man says, This is a clock shop, right? And she says, Sure. And he says, I want two hands and a face put on this thing."

Carol groaned. She almost divulged how her husband had told her lousy dirty jokes like that, but she decided not to go into him. He was dead.

Mama Gravy decided to try again. This isn't a joke that would be of interest to a gent, but I heard it in college so it's just for the gals. Three nuns are walking and talking on their way to school where they teach, and one says, I was cleaning the Father's room and I found that he had drawn some dirty pictures of a nun with her pulling her robes all the way up to her nose, showing all her private parts. The third nun asked, So what did you do? The first nun said, So I cut them to pieces. The second nun then says, And I was also cleaning in Father's room and found that he had a box of rubber prophylactics. The third nun asked her, So what did you do?" The second nun says, I poked holes in them all. The third nun fainted."

Carol frowned. "I don't think I like jokes of a sexual nature about religious figures. There's something unseemly about that. It seems unfair somehow."

Mama Gravy rolled her eyes. "That's the point of dirty jokes. To shock. If you don't want to hook your gents in with dirty jokes, then you can just try the come-hither peepers. Every star has her come-hither looks down pat. Your work here will help you learn how to do your peepers like a star."

* * * * *

At four in the morning, Mama Gravy steered an exhausted Carol to a top bunk.

"Etienne! Scoot your fat ass."

"Who? Wah? Oh crap." Etienne, with a bony behind, rolled over to face them. "I don't wanna share."

Mama Gravy told her, "You knew you would when I got a new girl on. Now scoot."

Etienne frowned and slipped toward the wall. After Carol grinned her best apology, she hopped up.

Etienne asked, "Are you a homosexual?"

"No."

"Good. Sometimes when I go to bed, I'm tired."

Carol agreed. "I'm dead tired, now. I could sleep a week."

"Good luck."

Carol moaned. "My feet are so sore I wish I could take them off and keep them in the other room."

Etienne said, "And when your feet get so tired you just want to die, there's only one thing you can do."

"What's that?"

Etienne chuckled. "Suffer. Suffer and pray that you just drop dead and are put out of your misery."

"Oh I'm so tired! I'm so tired!"

"Don't be so Dorthy Lamour down a volcano."

Carol asked, "What's that mean?"

Etienne explained, "Repetitive."

Carol was still confused. "Huh?"

"Well she's done it for at least two movies, now. Just fell right in at the end. That's what they say. What do I know. I never saw none of her pictures. Those jungle island pictures are all wet, if you ask me."

Carol agreed. "You and me both."

Several women hushed them and so they quietly drifted off to a deep sleep. That morning there was a violent thunderstorm that went on for over an hour and shook the walls. Carol did not wake up. It would have been like waking the dead.

* * * * *

Carol met many men and types of men during her dancing. Some wanted to talk about their mothers.

"My Mama! She made the best johnnycakes. They were so good! The best johnnycakes you could ever hope to have!"

Carol moaned, "Ooooh, you're making me so hungry."

Some men talked about their wives.

"I want to kill her! She's a monster right out of the fairy tales. She's worse than that. She's not in a book. She's in my house! If I don't kill her, I'm dead. The both of us can't be alive on the planet at the same time! She's pure evil!"

Carol suggested. "When she comes home so drunk that she can't even crawl straight, put a pillow over her face so that she can't even breath. Then she's dead."

"She don't drink."

"Oh. Then I guess you're stuck with her."

Some men were fired up to share their politics.

"The conservatives in America are the cause of this new trouble in Europe – this new trouble with Hitler!"

Carol said, "But I thought America wasn't involved with all that over there."

He said, "But the right wing of this country encouraged the trouble. They don't mind Hitler. He's against the Reds just like they are. And they allowed all this to happen by not ratifying the Treaty of Versailles and by not supporting the League of Nations, keeping it from ever having any legitimacy. So Hitler was never nipped in the bud. A strong League of Nations may have been able to do what it was made for. A weak League of Nations doesn't even have a chance to try. So the world ran off crazy all on its own as if no lessons were learned from that last horrible war. Italy was never nipped since then. Japan was never nipped since then. The best way to defeat Hitler isn't now but before he even got a chance to get started so many years ago. The conservatives would not lift a finger to stop him and now we got a monster and now we got a war. Conservatives love that part. They can only think to do things with war."

"Oh, that's all so far away."

"But you have to get mad! If you know what's going on in the world, you have to get mad!" He got louder. "How can you be awake and alive and not get mad!" He began to shout. "Get mad! Get mad! Get mad! The conservatives and right wing idiots have caused all this new war by not really dealing with the last war! So they can have another war! War is all they can do! Get mad!"

"I'm Carol Pan. I'm going to be a star. My name is going to be all over in lights."

"Get mad! Get mad!"

* * * * *

The next day, Mama Gravy painted a sign and hung it on the wall. No talking politics. No exceptions.

* * * * *

The next evening during a five-minute break, Carol spotted a mention in the newspaper about a cactus show sponsored by the CAC, the Cactus Appreciation Club. What caught her eye was the part that said they were planning to serve free roasted cactus and iced cactus juice as part of the festivities. Her stomach had been growling. She asked a woman on the bench next to her, "You can eat cactus?"

"I suppose."

Carol asked, "Is it good?"

She shrugged. "Depends on how hungry you are. They say hunger is always the best seasoning."

"What?"

"If you say that if you don't like something – you ain't really hungry at all."

Carol asked, "Sure. But won't this prick your mouth?"

"I suppose they figure out a way of getting rid of the pricks."

Carol marveled, "I didn't know you could even eat cactus. Jimmy Crickets."

"You learn to eat all sorts of things out here."

Carol nodded, to agree. "You and me both."

The woman said, "That reminds me of a joke: How is working for the film studios like going to bed with a porcupine?"

"I don't know."

"It's a hundred pricks against one."

Carol said, "That's not funny. I'd love to get into the studios and to get in all because my name's on their list at the front gate. Or better yet, they just know me because I'm a star so they all blow kisses and don't even have to look at a list." She looked at her paper again. "Cactus ketchup? Is that one of Heinz 57 varieties? Do they make that many different flavors of ketchup?"

"I suppose so." The woman took the paper. "They need all the flavors they can come up with, I suppose. I heard tomatoes won't be used anymore for a ketchup. Too expensive to grow. That was one of my favorites, along with mushroom ketchup. I like walnut ketchup, too. But if tomatoes start becoming too rare, I guess they'll start having to say they only have 36 varieties, soon."

"Sure."

The woman gave the paper back. "Have you ever tried grape ketchup?"

Carol answered, "Nope."

"Cucumber?"

"Nope."

"Fish, even?"

"Nope."

The woman rolled her eyes in disbelief. "You haven't used any kind of fish sauce in your life? That's the most common sauce. You never?"

Carol admitted, "I never had any kind of ketchup before. I only just heard of it. That's all. I see all the different bottles displayed in the restaurant windows."

"Your mama never made it?"

"We raised sheep. I don't think they'll ever make ketchup out of sheep."

"No. Not ever! You got to try some kind of ketchup, someday, just to say you did."

Carol agreed. "When I get rich enough, I can even buy nice shiny glass bottles of all 57 varieties! I'll put a drop of it on everything."

The woman stated, "If they start to make it out of cactus, the price of that kind better be cheaper. It don't take all that work to grow cactus."

Carol said, "You bet. Cactus will certainly replace the tomato."

Mama Gravy walked by. "Are you girls talking about food again? Every time I walk by all I hear all my girls talk about is food."

Carol said, "We're always hungry."

Mama Gravy replied, "Break's over. There's men lining up out there to make like the milkman at you."

Carol grumbled, "Isn't she a pill."

Mama Gravy added over her shoulder, "And don't take any wooden nickels."

* * * * *

The next afternoon when Carol woke up, she went to the drug store and counted out her pennies to buy a can of hair shellac. When she got home, she pulled on the big ugly crepe bridesmaid dress, and then heavily applied the hair glue. She had a picture of Norma

Shearer before her, to guide her. When Etienne opened the door, she exclaimed in alarm, "What's that smell? Is that your hair?"

Carol fanned herself. "I'm sure the smell will go away. It's part of this shellac."

"Is that the right kind to put in your hair? Is that Brilliantine?"

"I couldn't afford that so I got this Shinelli. I think it's for my hair. It sure ain't eyewash, that's for sure. It smells like a gas station, doesn't it?"

Etienne agreed. "Maybe it's something they put in it to help it dry faster. It'll take you about a week to dry, with all you're putting in."

Carol wanted to cry. "I can't get it right. I want it to be slicked down just like Norma Shearer."

"You going to a party? I hope so. You don't want to try so hard around here."

"Yes. There's a cactus show. I've been told I need to make a splash somewhere out where the press can see me, if I'm going to be a star, and maybe there'll be a camera there. That's how you become a star. You first got to be noticed somehow. And there's food."

Etienne was intrigued. "A cactus show? I'm in a magic show."

"I didn't know that."

"Sometimes. I was cut in half. It was a trick of course. Ireland the Magician did it real good. He says he's going to do it next time with a big round sawmill blade with long sharp teeth. And it's real. I'm going to be a magic act star someday, you bet. Ireland and I are going to hit it big. I only work here to make some money since he can't afford to pay me yet. But his new sawmill blade will put him on the map, because it's ferocious, and then we can tour the world."

Carol was jealous. "Wow. A magic act star. I hope this cactus show opens up something for me. Who knows? I read about it in the paper. They'll have refreshments. Cactus refreshments. It's all very modern. You want to come with me? It'll be fun."

Etienne looked oddly at Carol's dress. "You want press wearing that? You look like a piñata that's been whacked clean of all its candy."

"The pictures in the paper are all black and white so they'll never see what an awful shade of color it is. And if I'm looking right at the camera, it won't see this stupid fabric all bunched up behind me like this. I feel like I got a whole extra person back here. I wonder why they did that. Is that French or something?"

"The party is tonight?"

Carol answered. "No. In an hour. Will I ever get my hair right by then?"

"You can't where a long dress in the day. Only at night."

"The stars do."

"But that's different. They're in special costumes for special events. And they wait until nighttime, don't they, to wear the long gowns?"

"I never thought about it. I was just thinking they always wore long gowns."

"I don't know."

Carol said, stubbornly. "Well, they'll just have to take me as I am."

Etienne surmised, "And I bet, being a cactus thing, it'll be outside?"

"How'd you guess?"

"Then don't worry about your hair. Wear a hat. A lady is supposed to wear a hat during the day. Unless she's at home."

Carol began to weep. "But I spent so much money on the junk so I could look glamorous like a movie star."

"You look like a cow pie."

Carol agreed. "And what kind of a hat could I wear with this dress, anyway?"

Etienne said, "I have the perfect thing. This big straw hat. Now don't think you can wear all us other girl's things everyday. If they can't get all the details of Communism right over there then what makes you think we're any better with it at the dancehall. Plan on always wearing your own clothes. But I'll make this exception for such a special event."

Carol's eyes widened. "It's an odd color for this dress. Isn't it? I guess any color would be odd for this dress."

"Since color isn't an issue for you, who cares if it clashes."

"Oooooh. Etienne. You sweetheart. You'd let me wear that? It's so nice of you."

"Now you look like Scarlett O'Hara."

Carol frowned. "Oh, I'm not sure if that's a good think these days. The movie of that book is coming out at the end of the year and there's already rumors that it's a stinker."

Etienne said, "Really?"

"Yes. I read that the director of the movie turned down the chance to make a percentage of the profits. He just wanted a lump sum, upfront. He told the producer, who was trying to chisel him, that he thought Gone With the Wind would be the biggest white elephant of all time. If the director says that, you know it's a movie that no one will come to."

Etienne nodded. "Yep. I say, always get your money up front. Or you'll never see it."

"You and me both."

"Well, I guess we have until the end of the year to wear this hat. Then the look will have been ruined by a bad movie. I'll have to get a new hat."

Carol nodded to agree. "It'll be all wet."

"A flood."

When Carol hurried down the narrow hallway, her skirts loudly rustled against the walls like dry newspapers. She unhappily thought, "This thing is so noisy it must have been made for the silent era."

* * * * *

Carol hopped on the Santa Monica Boulevard line heading towards Silver Lake and soon the nun got on and sat by her.

Carol beamed. "Sister Agatha of the Streetcar! It's so wonderful to see you again. And your robes are so clean all the time. How do you do it? You practically glow."

"Do I, Carol? I see you glow from within today. You must have been praying. Boy you glow."

"Not really. But I've been wanting to be a star, real bad. Have you been praying? Oh, of course you have. You're a nun."

"I have been praying for Oklahoma."

Carol put her nose in the air. "Oh. The immigrants. And it's very dirty over there."

"That land is now a vast sea of dust. It is the valley of death. Fierce waves of heat blow over the face of the earth as if God has abandoned it. The Virgin weeps as she sees how the Earth of life and green plants has withered. Only the bones of herds give detail to the white dust. And just outside Lawton there's the bones of a little girl who got lost. There is nothing sadder and I have been praying for her. The cola bottles around her have become buried in the blowing dust and only the top of her bones stick out - only a few tips of her ribs and a small circle of her skull at the top of her pretty little forehead. Tonight I will go to her and help her into the hands of Mary, who always has room for all the departed lost children on her lap. Even the ones that have been withered into bones."

Carol frowned. "How will you get there?"

"On my broom."

Carol imagined a nun flying on a broom and belted out a laugh. "You're funny!"

Sister Agatha of the Streetcar chuckled along with her and then asked, "And what's your bowl for?"

Carol held her bowl up. "A cactus! I'm going to a cactus show! I'm going to be a star! Do you want to come with me? Can nuns go to things like that?"

"Certainly. I love agricultural shows. And I love dog shows and most of all I love food and wine shows. I love to walk the vineyards. But I have many sad people to pray for today."

"No praying for me," Carol boasted. "I'm not sad at all today."

"Wonderful. Then we'll pray a happy prayer."

"There's a prayer for happiness?"

The nun nodded. "That's when it's fun to pray."

"Do you have a happy prayer to me?"

"Certainly." Sister Agatha of the Streetcar closed her eyes and smiled. "The Lord is my shepherd; I shall not want. He maketh me to lie down in green pastures. He leadeth me beside still waters. He restoreth my soul; he leadeth me in the paths of righteousness for His name's sake."

"I grew up with a lot of sheep. Did that make me a shepherd too? Like the Lord is my shepherd?"

Sister Agatha of the Streetcar tapped the side of her gleaming white habit and wimple. "Yes. So you understand sheep. You understand more than you realize."

Carol spotted a road sign. "Oh! I better jump off here! I have to – " With no time to explain, Carol hopped off the streetcar.

Before Carol walked the rest of the way to the cactus show, she dug one up along the way to bring with her. She was assuming that's what one did for such events.

Behind a row of palm trees, she could make a big billboard for In Name Only. Carole Lombard's giant gorgeous face looked over the town like a comforting goddess. "I look as good as you! Well, almost. But I would if I was painted up so high like that. I'd spit in your eye if you weren't up so high!" She liked her poetry. She smiled pleasantly upon entering the sandy field behind In-N-Out Burger. She smiled pleasantly toward the gathered crowd of about one hundred, even though her fingers were pricked and she didn't feel pleasant about that. She hungrily regarded the large pile of glowing coals heaped on the ground. Over it were racks waiting for the green food to grill. She prayed they would change their mind at the last minute and decide to grill fat juicy steaks and potatoes for everyone, instead of something as weird and modern as cactus. She prayed hard, adding, "And I know a nun so you better listen." Then she handed her heavy cereal bowl to the first man she saw.

He didn't take it, but looked at the sand still spilling from the side of it in amusement. "You love cacti?"

"W-what?" Carol looked around. "Who's that?"

"Cacti. More than one cactus."

"Oh. I'd think that would be cactuses."

"No. The Latin is cacti."

"Oh. That explains why I wouldn't know that. I'm not Latin. I grew up in Montana. Up there a sheep-I would be something that looked at you. Get it? Eye. A sheep's eyeball." She laughed nervously and overtly winked a few times. "But give me a Latin beat and I'll be anything you want me to be." Carol felt stupid and regarded the two long rows of cacti already on display. Where do I put my entry?"

"Why did you bring a - a specimen?"

"Isn't this anything like the county fair? I once won a prize for having a basket of well-grown cucumbers. Third prize. I was so thrilled. Here's a cactus. See? Ain't she purdy? I think she kind of looks like a pig if you look at her from this angle. See? A real whiz-kid!"

"Do you have an entry form? An entry fee?"

Carol paused. "Oh." She looked at the others. "Did they?"

"No. But they're not so wet behind the ears. They're from esteemed members of the club, already, and the real point of this gathering is to promote a special line of cacti as the world's next food source. I don't think yours is very tasty."

"What's wrong with steak."

"These things can grow in the desert. They get most of what they need from the sun. After the war destroys Europe and its farms – and it seems like it's all coming hard and fast – the world will need new food sources and America's deserts are ready to produce."

"Yours are really keen to eat and mine isn't?" She gave hers a dirty look.

"These cacti here are special breeds that are sweet and tender, for eating. Is yours a special edible bred? No. It's a weed, for all purposes. It looks a bit – wee – "

A woman in a very lovely hat walked up to them. She glared at Carol's inappropriate dress length for time of day, and asked of Carol's offering, "Is that for our little gathering, here?" She mock pouted in Carol's bowl. "A sad little muffin."

Carol smiled at her. "I brought it for you to sit on. It's hot out here and you all can get tired. I brought it just for you." She held her cactus out to the woman. It flipped out of its bowl, not being very well anchored in the loose sand, and fell at their feet. They all gave it a horrified look as Carol added. "Careful. It bites." She tossed the bowl aside and pulled a needle out of her finger. "Lovely."

The two left Carol alone. She was now snubbed. But that didn't matter since boring speeches soon began.

"Blah blah – of the family Cactacceae – class Magnoliopsida – the largest genus is Opuntia – fruit common in Mexican markets – blah blah blah."

An hour later, after everyone's ears had been numbed by a blow of showy Latin and unassailable facts, the time came for the press and for everyone else to sample cactus juice. Big blocks of ice were wheeled out from a truck, chunks were chipped off and dropped into tumblers, and a lime green juice was poured in. After Carol had downed hers, not caring how it tasted, she decided it was time to get the press interested in her. She wailed out a big high note, did some boisterous tap dancing in the sand, and added, "Mammy! How I love yah!" She repeated it a few times.

The photographer did not move to snap her picture for his paper.

She did it again and started sweating bullets, realizing she should have worked harder on planning her script. It wasn't everyday the likes of her was in the company of a camera and she was blowing it. She danced bigger, and sang louder, "Love ya! Love ya! Where'd yah get those peepers!" She heard a gasp. She wouldn't let that discourage her. Then she realized that it was because she'd backed up into the coals and the back of her ridiculous dress had dragged into it and she was now a blazing column of greasy flames. She quickly pulled her fluffy sleeves off, pulled down hard on the corset, and kicked out of the skirts. She kicked the pile of aside, and smiled like she had done it on purpose and was Houdini. But everybody now looked above her head in horror.

"Your hat!"

She tossed it aside, saying, "Whoopsie!"

They still were in horror and she felt an intense heat on her head. A furious orange greasy pillar of fire was shooting up off it. Then people tossed the contents of their tumblers at her head. Some only had ice left. It hurt, along with the growing second-degree burns. Carol decided it was time to call it quits, so she wiped the juice out of her eyes, smiled one last time, and then sidestepped in the general direction of the streetcar line, forgetting she was only in her underwear. But the woman who had snubbed her before the boring speeches now hurried up to her and took her arm.

"You're brilliant," she quickly said in Carol's ear, and then loudly announced so her voice would be heard over all the commotion, "This was a brave but necessary demonstration of the potent power of cactus juice to treat burns. I do hope you got all of this demonstration on film."

The photographer nodded, wide-eyed and awed. "I'm getting the Pulitzer!"

"If war breaks out in Europe, and we pray it doesn't, but it will, there will be terrible burns to treat. Burns are the most serious of all wounds. Burns are the most difficult to treat. Cactus has natural medicine in it that cools burns and promotes their healing." She turned to Carol. "How do you feel?"

Carol lied. "I was feeling very hot. But now I'm as cool as a cucumber. I mean cactus!"

They laughed and applauded.

Carol took a bow. The woman pulled her aside and asked, "Are you really okay?"

"I'd like a very cold bath. Can somebody drive me home?"

"No problem."

"And – since my stupid stunt ended up being a helpful stunt for you, can I have ten bucks for the dress?"

"That's a lot of money and it looked like it was past its sell-by date."

"It was a dress."

"Very well." The woman took Carol to her car and wrote her a check. Then the woman got just as shrewd. "And you will do an ad for us, and for the Burn Society, advocating cactus juice as a burn cure, also with this ten dollars."

"My face on a poster? Kippy!"

"Yes. I'm sure the pictures taken today will be in all the papers. It was all very flashy and the press is such a dupe for that kind of thing. They'll take a picture and print it if it's anything burning. Using your face on a poster with a testimonial to the power of cactus following the newspaper article might provide some continuity. Are you sure you don't need to go to the hospital? You might be seriously burned."

Carol wouldn't dare admit to the pain, now, since she suddenly remembered she hadn't eaten. Oh. I'm cured. And on the way home you buy me a burger." She nodded toward the In-N-Out Burger behind them. And some iced tea."

"Very well. A meal now, to show my good faith, and tomorrow a lawyer will stop by your house to have you sign the contract. Where do you live?"

"You'll see." Carol got in the car, smiling, realizing that she'd just hit the big jackpot. An ad for the Burn Society, and the CAC, both, could somehow be her foot in the golden Hollywood door. On the way home, she nibbled her burger, starting to feel sick, and she dribbled her iced tea on her head.

The woman did not act surprised when she dropped Carol off at the seedy dancehall - she was a good actress. She just reminded her, "Tomorrow. A lawyer."

"Aces!" Carol got in the door and fainted.

Chapter Five

Carol woke up, feeling on fire - and she was also shivering.

She heard Etienne's voice say, "What happened? Should we call the coppers? Maybe a doctor should stop by."

Carol said, "Don't you dare. It'll get in the papers and blow my story. I'm supposed to be miraculously healed. Cactus!"

"Well then, wear a hat when you blow your horn. The hair on the top of your head is just ruined. It might even scab up. You might even go bald up there for all time."

"You can buy hair with a few pieces of tin. Who cares. I'm gonna be a star. This story is going to be big." Carol passed out again feeling like her entire head had been stung by a thousand bees.

* * * * *

Carol woke up screaming, "I'm on fire! It burns!"

Mama Gravy said, "Give her some morphine. Help her. She's in pain."

"It burns! I'm on fire! Oh God help me!"

Etienne said, "No dope. None like that. It'll just make her an addict for the whole rest of her life. We can't do that to her."

"But she might die."

Etienne reasoned, "Then, Mama Gravy, you'd just be wasting your heroin."

"I suppose. But I hate to see her suffer like this. I'll blow some of this reefer smoke her way."

Despite the great pain, Carol passed out.

* * * * *

Carol woke up again to somebody saying, "This story is so big. Look at you like that on fire. What a picture!"

Her eyes had swollen almost shut so she had trouble seeing the many different papers brought to her, but she forced herself. "Oh my god, how did I survive? I am so very very much on fire!"

"You didn't. Well - almost not."

"I look like a forest fire."

"Yes, you do. I keep looking for Nero in the background with his fiddle."

* * * * *

Carol heard Etienne's voice. "And Ireland the Magician made such a fool of himself. I'm so upset. I want to be a magic act star but first you have to find a magician who doesn't try and tear the whole place down. He was going to cut me in half and he got this big round saw blade from a real sawmill in Minnesota and it had big long sharp teeth. It wasn't some rubber prop. It was sharp. And it came down on me but it was so heavy that it went crooked and it started to saw into the box in a new place and sawdust sprayed all over the front rows and it got in people's eyes. It was just terrible. And the noise. It was just horrible. And Ireland tried to grab it to put it back on track and almost got his whole arm cut off. It ripped open his sleeve all the way from here to here, and ruined his jacket and he doesn't have the money for a new one. It was just a terrible performance. I never realized it was so hard to be in a magic act."

Carol wondered if she was talking to her. Carol wondered if she was dreaming.

* * * * *

Eight days later Carol woke up again. "Where am I? What happened?"

"Good morning Hindenburg."

"What? What room is this? Why are you here?"

Etienne said, "Dollface, you're at the Gold Rush, still, and you're going to be alright, I guess. Lucky you." She laughed nervously.

"The Gold Rush? Still? How long? Oooooh. I feel like death warmed up."

"Warmed up. Sure. You've been out a few weeks now. You've been out like the President."

Carol could only remember a dream where a black cat was eating her face off. "How? Why? Here? You care for me? Why didn't you all just toss me into a ditch?"

Etienne said, "Somebody big is pulling some strings on your behalf. Maybe that lady who'd given you the ride home is doing this."

Carol remembered that woman had been in the dream and she had turned into a black cat. "Her? How do you know about her?"

"You've been talking in your sleep. You said she gave you the high hat. And then you went on about something else and you said you got a real crumb of a bozo to get into a car crash over you. You said he was only thinking about his giggle stick and he wasn't watching where he was going. And bam! And you said your pimp got shot in the back running from a copper. And you said you murdered your own husband with your own bare hands - and a pillow. And then you said that you used to spread out your honey cooler for all your six brothers. Boy are you a piece of work. And I thought I had a colorful biography, since I'd once dated Al Capone's cousin's triggerman's brother. Yes. I did. I almost rubbed elbows with true American celebrity. "

Carol was horrified, so she said, "Oh, that's not true. You know how people talk in their sleep about made-up stuff. I was just dreaming some old books and magazines, I'm sure. So what about that. I never killed nobody with a pillow. How stupid. But why would anybody be pulling strings for me?"

Etienne said, "Now they're very interested in you. Veeeeeery."

"How?"

"How'd I know? Who am I?" Etienne laughed mockingly at herself, and then called out toward the other girls, "Hey, Carol just opened her peepers. And I think she also woke up." She laughed again.

Mama Gravy shuffled in and shooed the other woman out. She asked Carol, "What's with you? Make up your fool mind. Get better or die so I can have my room back."

Carol was impressed. "I've been in your room this whole time? You really care for me?"

Mama Gravy made a sour face and went to a desk where there was a tall metal urn with a spigot. She lit some coals in a fancy ventilated chamber attached underneath it. "Don't be a genius. We're supposed to treat you halfway decent. They're paying me to keep you like a queen." She fit a ceramic kettle on top in a fancy metal ring. "I'll make you sassafras tea. It'll cure you of anything. It'll stimulate you. It'll make you sweat. It'll make you pee like you never peed before. Now that's healthy."

Carol admitted, "I've never seen tea made that way before."

"Don't go calling me a Bolshevik, but it's a samovar and it's how the Russians make tea. I only got it because there isn't room for an entire stove in here and I have to have my tea. This middle part has water in it. I heat the water from under here with the coals, and on the top I have a strong concentration of the tea in my pot. The pot gets hot from the hot water. After I pour some in my cup, I dilute it with the hot water from the spigot. They say the Russians take their samovars with them to the beach, since they have to have tea wherever they go. I wonder if they have sassafras tea in Russian. I bet not. It's tea made from the root of an American tree. It heals anything. I'll heal you. Don't worry. If you're strong enough to drink tea, you'll be just fine."

Carol repeated, "You really care for me?"

"So I like you, sure. I like you like I like Christmas when everything under the tree has my name on it. I never got so much dough for having somebody around who eats so little."

"Yeah. I'm starving. I could eat the whole cow."

Mama Gravy put her hand on Carol's forehead. "That's a good sign. But for starters it's cold soup broth and root tea for you. For starters."

"I want a cow!"

"Nothing rich or you'll throw it right back up, being so starved over all. Your stomach just won't handle anything rich in your condition."

Carol was puzzled. "Why are people paying to have me kept like this? I've never had anybody make anything for me before in my life."

"The cactus people are in on this. There was a lot of press about you having cactus juice thrown at your head during their weird little wingding. So, now they even got a press agent to push cactus miracles all the way up to the White House. "

Carol marveled. "Really?"

Mama Gravy said, "Not that I'm an expert on everything. I'm just a used whore dealer. We all thought that your going to a cactus show was a just trip for biscuits – a total waste of time. And look how it's paid off for me. I may be able to put a new roof on this sieve before it's all over – if you live."

Carol was confused. "My getting burned led to this? They care so much about my burns?"

Mama Gravy said, "Aren't you a genius. Here's the lowdown. They care so much that either you die and we keep it kibosh - " she put her finger to her lips. "- so their burn cure isn't embarrassed, or you live and you smile nice in a magazine about how good their burn cure works. It's that simple, and it's simple, really."

Carol brightened. "Me in a magazine? I'll be practically a star."

"It's that simple."

Carol darkened. "Nothing is simple."

"You're right. There's big money in it for them. They want a big government deal. There's a lot of money in it for them in having the whole American war department buying their special breed of cactus for when that awful crumb Hitler breaks out of his cookie jar and people start finding themselves on fire. That's what the cactus people think anyway. Like I care about what's going on in Europe. It won't ever touch us. The ocean is just too damn big. Believe me. I'm never wrong."

* * * * *

The next day, a wildly expensive 1938 Phantom Corsair came to pick Carol up from The Gold Rush.

Carol asked, "Oh my god! How much money did that car cost?"

The driver smiled wickedly, holding the door for her. "Twenty-four thousand dollars."

"Poison!" Hopping in the back, Carol yelled to those who'd gathered from the dancehall, "Did you hear that ladies? I'm getting into a twenty-four thousand dollar car! I'm sitting down! It's going to drive away with me still in it! Somebody pinch me!"

And if that wasn't wildly luxurious enough, it even had a radio in it. While Tommy Dorsey played, Carol watched the town go by outside her window and felt like she would pass out from being like such a star. When the car pulled up to a large white building, she jumped out before her driver could get to her door. She excitedly breathed in the air as if it was special.

When Carol got to the makeup chair that seemed just like a dentist's chair, she noticed in the myriad of mirrors that her eyebrows and eyelashes were gone. What was left of her hair was a wreath of barn straw. So a team of two experts in white smocks fussed over her. A cherry glow was glazed over her until she looked well fed and healthy. While a thick pink wax was being painted on her lips with a stiff brush, a lawyer came by and made her sign papers. He stressed, "If you don't tell the press how sick you really were from those burns, then we won't set you on fire, again."

Carol put her finger to her heavy lips. "You want me kibosh?"

"Very."

She tried to look around. "Who's doing all this? Really."

The lawyer only said, "Just call them philanthropists who care about the future of medicine, food, and water."

"Cactus water. Cactus food. Cactus medicine."

He nodded.

"Oh. Mama Gravy was right. Why didn't you just say? The

cactus people."

One of the makeup experts asked the others, "Finished?" They nodded.

Carol smiled. "I look like Jeanette MacDonald."

One of the makeup experts frowned. "I was going for something unique."

Carol smiled bigger. "Yes. I'm going to be my own star."

An Asian woman stepped up to Carol's chair and removed the white cap from her head. She held up a black rubber comb and said, "Oh, my. This will need a bit of corralling."

Carol agreed. "There was a fire up there. The Devil himself, I bet, was mad at me for something. You should have seen it! It isn't everyday you burn up like I did."

"Thank God."

"Thank the Devil. If it was the Devil who set me on fire, then I'm grateful. Look. I get lots of publicity now."

The Asian woman wagged her comb at Carol. "Don't ever be grateful to the Devil. He isn't particularity nice."

"Oh, I ain't afraid of no Devil. He can't be too bad."

"And why would you say something as daring as that?"

Carol decided, "If the Devil was bad, God would have burned him down a long time ago, right? God burns things down He don't like, right? And God don't like things that are bad. Didn't he burn down entire cities for not liking how the people in them behaved themselves?"

"Well – I guess."

Carol continued, "And God does what He wants. That's the point. Right? If you can't do what you want, then you ain't God. Right? I don't know - I'm no expert on God but I sure know He's the one with all the power to throw lightening bolts and brimstone and all that at bad manners and sinners and cities. The Devil is nothing as long as there's a God around. Hmmm. I wonder if God burned me down. No. Of course not. He wouldn't miss. God is perfect. If you weren't perfect then you couldn't be God. If I was burned down by God, I'd be dead – or a pillar of salt. Didn't that once happen to somebody? Oh, the classics are hard to all so hard to remember."

After working on Carol's hair for a while in silence, the Asian woman asked, "You worried about religion a lot?"

"Sometimes. And I worried all over again after I almost died. I almost didn't make it. I was ready to go into the Great Beyond. I was looking forward to it, too. It sounds nicer than the Great Depression. But I lived, and fiddlesticks to that, so I have to wonder what that means, too, I suppose. Hey, wait a minute. You look all Oriental and all, but you sound just like an American."

"Of course. I was born here."

"Really?"

"Sure. Of course. The U.S. hasn't allowed any Chinese or Japanese immigrants for many many years, now. Since the railroad has been built from shore to shore, they decided enough was enough and stopped all Chinese immigration for years. So we all sound just like Americans. We've been here for generations by now."

"Oh. Golly. How interesting. I didn't know any Orientals in Montana. There sure is plenty here in L.A."

"My forefathers came in at the west coast, and we all had our own version of Ellis Island, right here. That's probably the biggest reason were mostly right there."

"Oh really?" Carol asked, "Why are you all afraid of the Statue of Liberty? Does it look like a Chinese Devil?"

She laughed. "No. Don't be a loon. It's just that China and Japan are on this side of the world and the other immigrants are closer to that side." She added some swirls of fake hair to the top. "Don't you know your geography?"

Carol rolled her eyes. "I'm not sure about where anything is. Oh! Look at my head! You really know how to work with a big mess! My hair looks as organized as Norma Shearer's!"

"Thank you. I was afraid I'd just have to find you a hat. There. You're all done now. And I think you look much better than Norma. I could swear she's sort of cross-eyed."

Carol hopped up out of the chair, had her nose powdered again, and then was called to the set. It was a small plain glowing white backdrop in the center of a large dark soundstage. A hand model joined her. With her beautiful fingers with beautiful varnished nails the hand model held a small cactus pot up near Carol's face, so that in the shot it would look like Carol's hands. After two hours of posing, smiling, and trying her hardest to look refreshed, the cameraman said, "It's a wrap."

Carol was proud. "I was ticketty-boo, wasn't I? Just a peach!"

He nodded. "Just fine."

Carol was given an expensive well-made wig to wear out on the street, with the explanation, "So they think you're just fine."

Carol said, "But I am just fine. Aren't I?"

"We want everybody to think cactus juice even cures burnt hair."

Carol got a sinking feeling. "Will my hair ever grow back normal up there?"

"Will Hitler ever go kosher?"

"Does that mean no?"

"Who knows? You could get lucky. Hitler could get lucky."

Carol felt her knees go week, like she'd just been diagnosed with tuberculosis or leprosy or worse. "A lady's hair is her crown of glory."

"Then don't forget to put your crown on before you go out where others can see you."

Carol walked outside and the fancy car was gone. One of the makeup experts gave Carol fare for the streetcar. When she got back, she was greeted by a few who were waiting for her. "My aren't you getting fancy. A streetcar home. What will you think of next to outdo all the rest of us?"

Carol blew kisses. "It was a dream!"

* * * * *

In her room, Mama Gravy lit up a marijuana cigarette and invited Carol, "Hey, doll, come here and do some reefer with me."

"Oh. I don't know."

"You don't like to smoke?"

Carol admitted. "Even cigarettes make me so dizzy - and makes my stomach feel sick."

"This stuff's good for your stomach. Calms mine down every time."

Carol admitted. "But reefer makes my throat feel like it wants to swell into a big dry hay bale."

Mama Gravy looked at Carol like she'd never seen her before. "What? You big dope. And I thought you were so hardboiled. You never done dope? Jeez, I'm talking to a hardened tea-drinker."

Carol confessed, "But I did something they called a dizzy mushroom once."

"Oh? Was it? What happened?"

"I just went to the studio back lot and saw lots of sets they'd tossed." Carol described all that she'd seen. "And I climbed up on it. I climbed up on a dream dump. It was a very strange place. Alone and sad and so temporary."

"Dollface," Mama Gravy said with a laugh. "That was a trip all in your head."

"But it seemed very real."

"There's no one studio around here that has done those movies that would have those sets and props. And the studios don't usually share junk. Sorry."

"Oh. Well it seemed real. But it did seem odd. I don't like getting doped up. It's not real. My reality is unreal enough, as it is. I don't need any help for weird things to happen."

Mama Gravy asked, "So what do you do then to make yourself happy? Everybody has to do something. God knows happiness just isn't in the air we breathe."

The only thing that makes me happy, or helps me somewhat when I'm sad, is macaroni and cheese. Or spaghetti. I really like a big bowl of spaghetti with lots of red sauce. That can help a girl feel better about life. A lot better."

"Aren't you sweet."

Carol asked, "Can't you think of anything better than spaghetti? No."

Mama Gravy said, "The most joy I ever got in my life was being in Aunt Betsy's will. She liked me best, at least when the will was drawn up. Lucky I was only eight at the time. A little girl is sweet at that age. It wasn't much money but I got to buy this joint with it. I'd worked here and then when I was thirty I bought it from the lady who sold it when the stock market crashed. She was reluctant about selling it. And it had nothing to do with the Depression. She kept coughing up big chunks of her lungs. That's what brought her to the desert climate in the first place. She'd lived in St. Louis and said it was so damp there it could rot your lungs right out of you in a hurry. But then she finally found out what we all knew. She had tuberculosis and didn't have long in this world. God! If I bought this damn shack when I was thirty then that makes me almost forty by now! Oh fuck! Forty! Goddam forty! What am I going to do when I turn forty! That's too old to live this life. I never realized the years had gone by like that! Ten years of depression and it still went by too fast!"

Carol asked, "Where's everybody else from those good old days? I don't see any girls around here who look older than thirty – if that."

Mama Gravy explained, "Yep, you can't be here and be too old. Most of the gals just excuse themselves if they haven't already died off from gin, kooties, or dope. Or just getting themselves killed by an angry man who can't get his manhood stiff anymore. But not the girls I first worked with. All the girls from my time moved on together in one angry pack when they got too old to work it. The ones that survived now live in a camp in the Hollywood Hills, in the west, at Laurel Canyon, but out beyond where they haven't built anything yet. Houdini used to live in Laurel Canyon but that's where they have houses, all just on one side of Mount Olympus Street. These ladies went beyond all that - into the wild."

"It sounds frightening."

Mama Gravy nodded and continued in a tone of voice as if she was telling a ghost story. "The ladies sleep in a lean-tos and huts they built themselves and they eat what they can poach. I visited them after their first month up there and they were still like a gaggle of girl scouts trying to make their first pumpkin pie. Then I visited the camp about a year later, expecting them to all be gone, or worse, to all have leprosy. It seems to me that if you camp out too long on all that dirt you could get leprosy. But they were not only still up there but they were like a bunch of mean ole' Marines - as disciplined as any group of men in an army and at war. It was amusing to me."

"And no leprosy?"

"None. But then about five years ago I went up there, again. Those that were still there, about eight of them, were all running around naked and painting symbols on each other's bodies with mud, and praying to weeds and bushes, and really just giving themselves up to the devil. It was chilling. I only thought city folks went crazy over religion, but this was nothing like that, come to think of it. There was nobody on the radio trying to get them to send in money for their soul. It was like religion with no money involved at all. I'd never seen anything like it, I tell you. Is that Communism?"

"They'd gone mad?"

Mama Gravy added, "Actually, other than being naked, mud painted, and weed praying, they looked well fed and happy. They were doing something right. I wonder if that could last. I should go up there again someday and see if there's still anybody up there. One thing's for sure – there's not going to be any spring chickens up there. It's been ten years now. Oh, I'm a fainting daisy! Ten years! No spring chickens!"

Carol said, "Chickens eating bugs."

"What? Who said anything about poaching bugs? No, there's bigger game up there in the hills. But still, what a hard way to live for all those old gals. When you get old there's really nothing much you can do but get out of town. Even the camps in the hills aren't for the old people. The living is too hard. I wonder where old people go? This town is especially supposed to just be for the young people - young and beautiful and full of fashion and dreams. But sometimes you see a few zombies on Vine Street that used to be a working girl. If you ever catch her eyes all you see is a sudden flash of hate and anger. Never look a person in the eyes like that - especially somebody just standing around like that on Vine Street. It'll freeze your soul. Never look into the eyes of a zombie if you ever want to have peaceful dreams from then on out." Mama Gravy sucked on her reefer again. "God this stuff makes me talk too much. Sorry I don't have any spaghetti for you. I wish I had some for me. God, I could eat a cow. I could eat a horse. I could eat a cowboy." She began to giggle wildly.

Carol said, "That's okay. I'm not sad today."

Mama Gravy frowned. "You will be. It's hard to let men treat you like toilets and not get sad sometimes."

"Toilets?"

"Sure. Men are always pissing good money down the toilets. It might as well be you. Money's gotta go someplace. And seventy percent off all my money goes down the mob's toilet. They say they protect me. Ha. I bought this place with my own money. It wasn't much. But making it big in life ain't how much dough you have at one time. It's all in the timing. I don't deserve this place." Mama Gravy started to cry. "I was just at the right place at the right time with the right amount of money. I'm just a lousy punkola like anybody." She started to laugh. "I'm saying too much. A girl like you with such a sweet face makes me want to open up and spill my guts. I got to be careful. You may be scheming on how to take this place away from me. Maybe the mob sent you."

"Don't be a louse."

"But you like working here enough."

Carol admitted, "I like the company of women. I like that it's just us all camped out here - and it's us girls against the world."

Mama Gravy said in all seriousness, "Maybe you'd be better off being a nun. They all camp out together."

"I'm sure I'd like that. I really don't need to whoopee it up all the time to be happy. But I seriously think that being a nun would badly reduce my chances of ever being a star. That's the only reason

I'm here in this sinful town. I'm not here to count the lizards."

"You got me there. Stars are all sluts anyway. Nuns are really the ones who are them against the world."

Carol stressed, "And nuns don't become stars."

* * * * *

A week later while Carol was dancing with customers, Mama Gravy called her into her bedroom. A man was there.

Mama Gravy introduced her to him with, "I'm your agent now and I get ten percent of everything. Meet Mr. Chewing Gum."

Carol was appalled. "Ten? Why so much? That sounds like an awful lot!"

"It's hard work. And his name is really Mr. Daunner but he's in chewing gum."

He politely put his hand out to Carol to shake. "I'm so pleased to meet you. We'd like you to model with our new chewing gum that's coming out next month. Basil. It's really basil flavored. We think it'll be a big hit."

Carol smiled excitedly. "Because I'm such a star?"

He nodded. "I've heard of the ad you'll have out for the cactus burn medicine. We think your image will come to represent cool and refreshing. That's Basil gum. Cool and refreshing.

Carol frowned. "I thought that cactus ad should have come out by now. I've been banned from almost every magazine rack in the city, I've been looking for it so hard."

"Really? It hasn't come out? Hope it does. If it doesn't then your gum ad will be pulled as well. We only want somebody who is already associated with the image of cool and refreshing."

Carol bragged, "I've already been in the paper. I'm already a star."

He said, "Hot and bothered. On fire. Maybe we'll need to see if the cactus ad comes out before we even schedule a shoot for the gum."

Mama Gravy stomped on Carol's foot, as she said to Mr.

Daunner, "Don't wait. Pay up now. Shoot her tomorrow. Don't wait or we just might get a better offer from somebody else to peddle cool and refreshing and we won't be available to you and you'll feel all wet."

"I'll first check out when the other ad is scheduled to come out, and get back to you." He excused himself.

Mama Gravy yelled at Carol, "How could you have said something so stupid, you stupid idiot!"

"What?"

"You stupid idiot!"

"What did I say?"

"About the other ad not coming out yet. Of course it hasn't. Those things take months to make it through all the planning. Do you think a magazine is thrown together in a day?"

"I never thought about it. But don't worry. He'll be back"

Chapter Six

He didn't come back. The cactus ad never came out.

Carol decided, "Basil flavored gum sounds stupid anyway."

Mama Gravy ordered, "Your break is over. Dance."

"I just sat down."

"I don't care. I'm mad at you. Dance. And tell a dirty joke that burns a hole in their pants. Get them on the mattress so fast you get rug burns. And then you give me the money. Damn you."

Carol got up and went into the arms of a skinny awkward man. He asked, "How long have you been a dancehall hostess?"

"What did the frog say to the fly, while doing time in the big house?"

He just looked at her.

"Time's fun when you have flies."

"How long have you been working here?"

"Not long. And I'm also a star. I was on fire and was cured by cactus juice."

His eyes glimmered. "Oh, that was you?"

Carol smiled proudly. "And any day now I'll be in all the magazines in an ad promoting cactus juice. What line of work are you in?"

"I work at Republic."

Carol perked up. "The studio? The movie studio? The one where they make movies?"

"Yep. That Republic."

She was so excited she impulsively slid her hand between his legs. He didn't flinch. She realized what she'd done and was horrified. She didn't want to seem so hungry. She was a star. She pretended she hadn't done it and brushed at her own sleeve. "Oh – ah - I thought movie people didn't leave their little silver bubble and socialize with the rest of us little people over here in the dusty side of town."

He laughed and put her hand back between his legs.

Carol decided her hand needed to brush at her sleeve more as she asked him, "What do you do at Republic? Can you make me a star? I mean, I already am a star, but do you know if there's anything at Republic I should know about? That I could be in? Even a little part? Awe, come on, there has to be a part for me."

He thought it over and finally said, "I'm just an associate producer. A new project is being developed and the casting is going to be as cheap as they can get."

"I'm cheap. I'm really cheap. I'm a two-bit cheap star like you've never met before. And I can do anything." She let him put her hand back between his legs.

"I suppose."

With her other hand, Carol desperately waved Mama Gravy over to them. She came up to them angrily. "What. Did my idiot stomp on your feet? Or did she tell that goddam frog joke again that's so off the cob that the Okies can't even find it?"

"No," the associate producer defended Carol.

Mama Gravy continued, "Well my genius is capable of it."

Carol said, "It's an audition at Republic. And you're my manager. Or agent. So you should be there and earn your five percent."

"Ten."

Carol pouted. "I think that sounds so high."

Mama Gravy instantly ceased her anger. "A movie for our own rising star, Carol Pan. How lovely. You do realized she's had a lot of magazine coverage lately?"

"Oh?"

Mama Gravy lied, "And she just did an ad for Basil Gum. I bet it'll come out in a month or so. Everybody in town says Carol is soooo cool and refreshing!"

He said, "Oh? Well stop by the studio tomorrow and tell them I sent for you and I'll get you an interview with the producer if you'd like, but first, how much of a dancehall hostess are you?"

Carol nodded. "Very."

He pulled Carol tight to himself so she would feel his every little detail in his pants, and he said, "Well I've had enough dancing. I ain't a man of much patience. Where's your backroom?"

Mama Gravy grandly waved him toward the backroom. "This way, sir."

He told her, "I don't mind if I do. And this one will be free of charge, since I'll be doing you a favor tomorrow at the studio."

Mama Gravy reminded Carol. "Ten percent."

Carol quipped, "Wow. The casting couch has come to us." She thought about it and shrugged in satisfaction. "Kippy! Saves time!"

* * * * *

The next day Carol and Mama Gravy hitched north to the San Fernando Valley to find Republic. They got in a truck with an older man in a cowboy hat. He said, "I used to work there when it was still Mack Sennet's old studio back in the twenties."

Carol breathed in the fresh sweet air of the orange groves all around them. "Oh, those were funny films, weren't they?"

"It's a good studio."

Mama Gravy chimed in, "There's nothing like a burning stagecoach being shot at by arrows and guns and cannons before it goes over a cliff into the sea. They do everything up so fast and exciting at Republic."

He agreed. "Last thing I worked on was some stunt work for MGM. I was a DF back then, a dead fall, as they called us. That's what they call a western stunt man."

Carol said, "Fascinating. What were you working on?"

"We was all at Bob's Ranch getting ready to film some things with shootin' and carrying on. Then we saw Republic set up to film a few hills away from us. Some of us went over to ask about what they were doing. They said the covered wagons would be on fire as they came over the hill, being chased by about a dozen Indians. They were real Indians so they didn't need no expensive makeup and wigs. I think MGM would put an Indian wig on a real Indian just to waste money. Anyway, I looked at the three covered wagons and I said, Oh, you're going to have one covered wagon coming over the hill on fire, and these two others are for your next two takes. He said, No, we don't have any others for any other takes. It's all going to have to be done in one take So I went back to Bob's Ranch for some coffee and I tell you we watched them and we were very impressed with them, indeed. They had their shot in the can and they were gone before we even started rehearsing for the first take – before all of us had even finished our coffee."

Mama Gravy nodded. "Yes. I'd heard they were very frugal."

"So my advice to you. Little lady, if you want to make it at Republic, is to do it right the first time. Don't make them have to do several takes."

Carol agreed. "It wastes film. That sounds expensive."

"The most expensive thing on a shoot is time. I don't know what their unions are like over there, or if they even have any. But even if they don't, still, the most expensive thing about making their movies will be time. So always get it right the first time. Prepare. Be thoughtful. Be professional. Be fast."

"Thank you." The two women got out and still had a few hills of orange groves to walk through. Mama Gravy grumbled but Carol loved the landscape. They kicked out of their heels and walked barefoot through the warm dry sensuous dirt. When Carol got to the studio she noticed that it wasn't small, but it wasn't big, either. She was like Goldilocks finding something that was just right. The size made it seem warm, cozy and inviting. Like a family.

Carol also found that the men who made so many westerns were very healthy and that the work of the casting couch had to be repeated since the young strapping producer of the new project suddenly decided that he also had a charge in his gun that needed to go off. As he threw his jeans and shorts over the arm of the couch, Carol sighed, "My - aren't you plenty rugged."

"I'm just a Joe. I do cowboy pictures. This ain't no couch for big musicals. Just apple pie."

"What?"

"Lay back."

Mama Gravy waited outside the office door, and since her ear was to it she knew exactly when to come back in. "Is this a western? Is this a serial? Is this a bit part? How big? We like big things. My - aren't you plenty rugged. We like close-ups. We like lots of dialog. Carol is excellent with dialog, as you have heard how pleasant her voice is with your own ears. A real canary. They say she is cool and refreshing."

He agreed. "I feel so refreshed."

Carol smiled ear to ear. "Do I have the part? I was ticketty-boo on the casting couch. I know I was. Satisfactory services, and with a smile. I gotta get a part, now!"

"We'll find something for you, since you're so up and coming. We wouldn't want to pass up on that window of opportunity."

Carol smiled at her manager in exhilaration. "Mitt me, kid!"

Mama Gravy pretended to sock her in the jaw. "Yep! Congrats!"

The director finished buttoning his pants up. "Sweet. We'll be doing a remake of the old horror chestnut, The Face At The Window, this time as a western." He took his time with his socks and cowboy boots, and then he sat at his desk and pulled out some pieces of paper. "Since we're not spending any money on it, we won't have any real stars. We signed up a new nobody and a few old cowboys, already, who've been in our serials since day one, to do the final shootout, since we know that's the only way to end a Republic picture, but a starlet like you might do us some good. We'll lead people to believe you're up and coming."

"She is!"

He gave Mama Gravy a dubious glare, then continued to Carol, "And I can see your kisser will look good on the poster. But here's the lowdown. There isn't a real part for you in the script so we'll just have to make you into some doll on somebody's arm, if you want a part."

Carol gasped. "That's all? That don't sound too healthy a part."

He rubbed his lips. "Hmmmmm, We can put you as the girlfriend of a character played by Peter Fortune who was in A Face

In The Fog, if you remember. We'll make him the one who's dizzy for a dame. Yeah. That should work."

The two women nodded as if they knew who he was.

"Remember that one? Victory Pictures did it in 1936. At the end, Fortune is gunned down. I think I'd be good to give him a girlfriend in this picture. You can say how scared you are, blah blah blah, and maybe be the doll who always wants to dance, rat a tat tat, who has too much energy. You can give the picture some cocaine. It'll probably have a week to shoot but we haven't set that yet. We just know we'll make it a western instead of it taking place in Paris. The Brits have a version of it coming out this year with Tom Slaughter. The Face At The Window was first done as silents in 1919 and then in 1920. And the first time with sound in 1932 with Leslie Hiscott."

"But yours will be best, "Mama Gravy added as she tried to flatter him.

"Don't be a pill. Ours will be the cheapest yet, being a quick western with some old dusted off sets. We'll have to make sure there's a scene in our cave. We have a cave set out back that's just waiting to be used again and again. As a western, ours will have its charm and set itself off from all the others. It'll be good enough."

Mama Gravy said, "Sign her up for anything, at any price. Once her face is on a movie poster, it's a foot in the door."

"A whole leg," Carol corrected her. She looked at her own and envisioned it covered in Nylon. "A modern leg!" She grinned so big she looked crazy.

Mama Gravy held her hand out. "So. How for much dough for signing?"

He admitted, "The price is so low, there won't be any cash until we release it."

Mama Gravy's eyes hardened. "What? There has to be some money at signing. Let her sign the contract today. Give her some dough." She turned to Carol and pointed at her threateningly. "Ten percent!"

He put his hands up like he was being arrested. "We won't get a piece of tin for this thing until it's sold to a distributor. You'll just have to be patient and wait for any dough until then. And then it depends on how much we can sell it for and how cheap we made it and what the difference is."

Mama Gravy protested. "What a way-way minute! Woah! That ain't how movies are made. I happen to know they get money upfront, too."

"Maybe at MGM. The majors all got big banks out East and deep pockets at home. But not here, not for pictures like this. This is pure poverty row. This one's coming in under the bridge."

"What?"

"It's not on Republic's official roster until it's ready to sell. It's being snuck in without the rest of the industry knowing so we can release it with the other one, the British version, and use their press. And if there's any lawsuits, it'll be too late for them to do too much about it. By the time a cease and desist hit us in the balls, by then we'll have made all our profits."

Mama Gravy asked, "This picture could start a lawsuit?"

He nodded. "Before your very eyes. Most do. Especially if they make any kind of money. We always plan on lawsuits and plan on how we can be too fast for them." He turned to Carol. "Now I want you to come back tomorrow to meet the director. He's plenty rugged, too, so plan on an apple pie ring-a-ding-ding for him, too."

"Sure." Carol looked to Mama Gravy and crossed-her eyes in dismay.

* * * * *

On the way back, Carol said, "I'm so excited to be a star."

Mama Gravy groaned. "Now that your head has already swollen too big, are you going to want me to talk about how wonderful you are every minute? Am I to tell you how pretty and clever you are, even when you fall out of the squat hole every morning? Oh my! I bet she squatted like a star! God damn, Carol, to try and feed your ego is like trying to feed enough children to the gods of Babylon.

Now let's not make a meal of what should be just a swallow."

Carol made like an oyster and didn't say another word.

* * * * *

A Face At The Window took five days to shoot, at sixteen-hour days. It took so long to shoot for a B picture because they wanted to imitate Universal Studios monster movie lighting. For them to set up the lights different for each shot, so that sinister shadows would always be sliding across the back wall as actors moved took care and time.

Carol shot only one day, appearing in four scenes that would be separated by editing, but all taking place in the same set. An hour was wasted from the lean schedule when young nobody cowboy star Johnny Mayham correctly suspected that Carol was getting more close-ups than he was, making her his new rival. His ego was finally stroked with an extra long close-up for him, and fifteen minutes on the director's casting couch with his new rival.

When she got back for a medium shot, she said her final line, "I feel so – so – so ready for the booby hatch!"

"Cut! Perfect in one take! It's a wrap. Kill the baby."

Carol gasped. "Kill the baby?" She looked around in horror like there was about to be a human sacrifice to ensure the success of the project.

"A baby is that little spotlight. Kill it means to turn it off. Don't be so jumpy."

Carol laughed at herself and put her hands over her face in embarrassment. "Oh my giddy aunt!"

* * * * *

Then, to oddly offset the parsimonious production, there was an opulent cast party at the writer's villa. And he had quite a villa. Carol's first comment was typical of a first guest. "There's a dead horse in your swimming pool."

A full sized rubber horse lay on its side at the bottom of the pool for no reason other than the writer thought it was a funny idea and there was another writer who had one in his pool, also.

Carol asked him, while he spooned caviar in her face, "Why didn't you sneak me in a few more lines? It was my first picture and that was swell, and I'm not complaining, but I somehow feel like I got a bum steer."

"You don't want to reach too high on a budget that is so low."

"Really? Ah come on. Don't be so off the cob."

"Really." He poured her some champaign. "All actors feel like they weren't in a shot long enough. If the movie was three hours long and it was nothing but you, you'd still say, you didn't hold my shot long enough It's just how it is with everybody."

"Oh. You write anything else?"

"Most of what I write gets rejected. I just wrote a screenplay about communist bank robbers. I was told no communists. It was a great story about the struggle between labor and capital."

"You a communist?"

"I was when I wrote it."

"I don't understand."

"When I write something, I believe it when I write it. I can be a Jew, or a nazi, or a communist, or a tycoon, or a king, or a black slave woman with a stutter and sixty-three hemorrhoids. I believe it at the time."

Carol was utterly shocked. "A woman?"

"Yes. A writer has to be bisexual."

"You make whoopee with men, too?"

"No. I don't really go to bed with them. It's all in my head when I write. I believe what I write. And many times I'm required to write from a woman's point of view – if the character is a woman. So I become a woman in my mind."

Carol took a step back. "You're the one ready for a booby hatch."

He nodded to heartily agree. "Yes. A writer worth his salt is always deep in his own booby hatch."

Carol asked, "What else did you write about?"

"It doesn't matter. Cowboys are where it's at. It's all lies, but that's okay. Myth is myth and America needs its myths like any place else. The Nazis are spinning yarns about coming from a race of super men who were a master race who were twelve-foot giants. So they got a handicap there - now that's hard to film on poverty row. Cowboys can be filmed on poverty row. A horse is cheap. A desert is cheap. A shootout is cheap. And so much fun."

Carol was confused. "You mean there weren't really cowboys?"

"Yes. But not like the movies have them. And all our cowboy trappings and culture originated in Mexico, but the movies would have you think they're in sombreros and ponchos and it's two different people and cultures, completely."

"But what were the real cowboys?"

"People who herded cattle from the east to west for the cattle barons - who were usually Europeans just out to make a buck off of this new land. The giant herds trampled the fences and crops belonging to the real new Americans, the homesteaders. The cowboys shot all the buffalo herds in their way, ruining the Native American way of life for them. But the myth favors the cowboys and makes him out to be the hero. But all a cowboy really did was destroy all that was really American. That's the real story. He was really the cattle baron's thugs - just thugs to protect European investments. But you don't know that from going to the movies. You never get the truth. You get what was bought by those with the power. And so when they sing about how they love the cowboy, at Republic, it's just code for I love the Conservative Party."

Carol grabbed his arm and laughed. "Oh, you sound like you're getting political again. Just write a story where the cowboy shoots the bank robber or the Indian and saves the saloon lady and you've got a winner. That's not politics. That's just a good story."

"You're right. Don't think. Write." He looked around at his fancy massive home. "This town certainly pays you enough to do just that."

* * * * *

Carol Pan went back to being a dancing hall hostess. She waited and waited. The British version of the film came and went and there was no sign of Republic's version.

"What's going on, I wonder?" Carol cried to a very angry Mama Gravy.

"Let me find a horn and talk to some criminal producer prick at that studio and I'll find out everything." Mama Gravy found a phone booth and dialed up the studio.

She found out that a lawsuit had come early from Radio, the British company, against Republic, and the American print was not only shelved, but had already been burned.

Mama Gravy cried, "Burned!"

"We snipped the end off of it, first. The shootout on horseback at the end was original, so we shot a new picture with those actors to go with it. A Face In The Dust."

"And bring Carol back. Add her scenes back! You can find some arm to have her hang off of. I just know you can! This is her big break!"

"Sorry. It's already all in the can."

"Why don't you want me to get my ten percent? Why? Can't I buy a little happiness just once in my life? You're despicable. All of you out here! You ruined this nice place. It was a shame to take this country away from the rattlesnakes and replace it with something worse! Rotten egg men like you!"

He had hung up but she continued.

"There's nothing wrong with this place that a couple of funerals can't fix! How dare you do this to us! How dare you! No matter how all you directors and producers try and dress things up, this town is nothing but a big machine that puts skin on baloney! And you can choke on it! And you can choke on all of it at the same time!"

Mama Gravy paused only when she noticed that some of the glass panes in the booth were cracked, and she didn't think they had been before.

* * * * *

Carol was dancing a bit sluggish the next day. She said with a low moan to one of her partners, "I just wanted to be a star. Is that too much to ask? That's all I wanted. I just wanted to be a star."

The man said, "It's a rotten town, isn't it?"

"I just wanted to be a star."

The man said, "Well, you know what they say, to be a star you need the stamina of a cow pony."

"I could pull the dead weight of a hundred Norma Shearers. I'm box office."

"Sure kid."

"Big box office. I just know it if I had the chance. I know some people say trying to be a star is harder than chasing a fart through a bag of nails, as they say, if you pardon the expression, but still, I just think if I had the chance – if I only had the chance. Once people saw my face glowing up on the big screen they'd know what they got. And I got a good voice, too. I tell you, I'm up to mustard. I really am. For a while there my career was going like a real cliffhanger. Now it all just seems to have hit a brick wall. A brick wall that ain't budging for nothing."

"Can I lick your briskets?"

"Backroom. It'll cost you a quarter."

When he left, Mama Gravy said to her, "You must be beat. Just beat up. You poor doll. I've been feeling bad for you and I usually don't tear myself up over other people's bad luck, but dollface, you've really gone through bad luck like a dose of salts."

Carol frowned. "I don't know what I can do about it. I wish I could just biff it in the nose and make it go away. Go away, bad luck! Go away!"

Mama Gravy said, "It's been a terrible week. I think it's time I shared some of my punookee with you. I think it's gotten that bad."

"Punookee?"

"My dragon. My morphine. It's the only thing that calms me down when things get so bad that I can only think of death."

Carol had heard too many bad things about morphine. She wearily shook her head. "No. I'm too sad for anything. There's only one thing that can be done now."

Mama Gravy cried, "Don't jump off the Hollywoodland sign. Oh please. Don't do that. You're still so young."

"No. No. There's only one thing that can be done. Lots and lots of spaghetti. A big bowl of it. That's the only thing that could make me happy, now. And a bottle of that red wine that comes in a basket. That could make me feel better, too."

Mama Gravy paused to think of it. "That helps. Yes. It does. Come to think of it, that sounds pretty good." She licked her lips.

"And meatballs. Not those puny hard white little Swedish meatballs but those big fat juicy black eye-talian meatballs! Made with black olives."

"My. You know a lot about those things."

"I've had spaghetti once before and it made me very happy. And I've heard about the meatballs you get at an eye-talian restaurant. I've gotta go find it. I gotta just gorge. I want to be happy!" Carol broke down crying. "That's all I want is to be happy. I'm not happy!"

"You poor dear. You go find some darling little bistro and eat yourself silly. Yes, there is something magic about spaghetti that makes a person feel better. You go right now."

"It's late. Do you think I'll find one that's still open?"

"I don't know. Just get on the streetcar heading someplace nice like toward Hollywood Boulevard and ask around about it and see where you're pointed. Who knows? You might find a bistro that's open and you might get to eat spaghetti! Who knows? It's a insane town!"

* * * * *

Just off La Brea Avenue near Hollywood Boulevard, Carol sat at a charming small table by herself that was covered in a cozy red check tablecloth. A candle in a green glass jar flickered. She poured another glass of red wine from the bottle in a basket.

A swarthy man sat down opposite her. "You shouldn't eat alone. You're too pretty."

"I don't think there's any black olives in the meatballs. Aren't they supposed to do that? These don't have any. "

He shook his head. "Not usually. Mama used to make them that way. My brother loved them so much. But meatballs aren't usually made that way. How odd you should say that. I'm in town looking for him. He just came to Hollywood and then disappeared."

"Oh. Really. Well, anyway. A man named Ramon Classic used to tell me that the best way to make meatballs – "

"That's my brother!"

"Ramon?"

"Yes! Yes! Where is he?"

Carol frowned. "He was shot."

"What?"

Carol nodded. "I was there. He ran from a copper and he was plugged in the back."

"What?"

"Yep. Shot full of daylight."

"Oh my God. Oh sweet Mary. Oh my poor brother! I'll kill whoever it was who did that to him!"

Carol repeated. "It was a copper. He was running. He wouldn't stop. I was there."

"How did you know my brother?"

"We was. You know. He and I. We was working the streets."

"You a working girl? You have a new man to take care of you?"

"No, I don't have a man in my life right now. I got a gal to watch over me. Now I'm just a dancehall hostess."

"Be my dollface. Be my girl. I won't make you work the streets. I'll buy you nice things."

"How many girls you got in your stable by now?"

"Only three. But I bet you'll be the one who lasts."

"If you want me that way, I don't share. But I promise you, I can do three different things to you in bed better than anybody else. You won't miss out on that department."

His eyes bugged out and he looked around the bistro to see if anybody else had heard her say that. "My you advertise your movie like a studio executive."

Carol agreed. "It's Hollywood. You got to sell hard. Sell fast. Hit below the belt. Sell before the next guy. Try to sound original, even though you ain't."

"Okay, I'll tell my dolls on the side to hit the road. It'll be you and me. I'll just need you to help me find the copper who plugged my brother. I need to chop him into little bits and feed him to the fishes. He needs to pay for what he did to my brother."

"I'll have to think about it. I'll have to eat more spaghetti and that'll help me think."

"What is there to think about? You be my girl and we kill that crumb."

Carol pouted. "It's just hard to think. You know how it is. With all that's happened. And happened so fast."

"Take your time. And the bill's on me. Then come to by bed and show me those three things that are your specialty."

"I don't like to be used."

He said, "Sure. I ain't no crumb. And then in the morning, meet my family. I think they'll love you. I hope. You don't happen to have any Sicilian in you?"

"What's that?"

"Southern Italy."

"No eye-talian in the least. Swedish, Polish, Ukrainian and German. And there have been claims that there's a French man in there somewhere. I'm a real American mutt."

"Well, I'm pedigree Sicilian. With a little Dutch thrown in from Grandpa on Mama's side. He liked to travel. And I think we also have some Portuguese. But I don't think I look Portuguese in the least. And don't say Italian like that. Eye-talian. Sheesh. It's Italian."

Carol carefully said, "Italian."

"Very good."

Carol asked, "Oh. And now that we're almost married, what the hell is your name?"

"Antonio Caltanisseta."

"Caltanis – "

" – setta. Caltanisseta."

"Oh my. It won't be the first time I had an awkward last name."

"What the hell is awkward about Caltanisseta? As a baby, they say it was the first word I said. And how many other last names have you had. How many husbands do you have that are going to come back and give me trouble?"

"Just one and he's dead."

"Did you bump him off yourself?"

"What?"

Antonio squinted at her accusingly. "You look like the kind of dame who'd bump off her own husband if it would get her a nickel."

Carol jolted, feeling like Karin again. "Don't be a twit. Do you have a car?"

"Just got one this week. All us Caltanisseta brothers are working fast here in Hollywood. Almost all of us have our own cars by now. By next year we'll own the town."

Carol asked, "How many brothers do you have?"

"There was seven of us altogether. My sister died when she was little. She starved. And now my brother, Ramon."

Carol thought about how that was same number of kids as her family. She hoped his didn't involve incest, though. "Drive me home, I'm ready to go."

Antonio frowned. "Aren't we going to my place? My bed? Your three tricks?"

"You really want to marry me? You just met me. Are you sure that ain't as silly as a hat full of worms to be talking like this?"

"Sure I'll marry you. Why not? I need to get married to somebody who looks like you so I'm not just thought of as a WOP. I need a social secretary. I need a nice blonde woman on my arm to show the world I made it. You look mighty blonde."

Carol nodded. "There you are. You and me both. The studio bosses all married blonde women and changed their own names, even, to not be Jewish anymore. It just seems to be the thing everybody's trying to do around here. I don't know why but it sure sells a lot of peroxide to want to look Republican."

Antonio said, "Baby, you may have been a harlot but I wasn't terribly well-heeled in society, myself. We both need a ladder rung up and we can use each other. It's okay to use other people when they use you right back. We're building each other's empires. That's a marriage. Let's go to bed. With a wife, you get that, too."

"Don't get your balls in an uproar." Carol held her belly and frowned. "Not right now. I'm much too full of spaghetti and wine. I'm ready to fall asleep right here."

He saw that it was true and stood and took her arm. "Alright, doll. And then I'll pick you up at noon and we find that copper and I blow his face off."

Carol reminded him, "We visit your Mama, first. We get married first. Then we can be a team and do all kinds of things that take two."

"Italian women aren't like you. I like that."

Carol nodded proudly. "Welcome to Hollywood."

Chapter Seven

The next day on the ride to Mama Caltanisseta's apartment, Carol asked, "This car looks new. How much did it cost?"

He chuckled. "You always ask people that?"

Carol opened and closed the glove compartment. "I'm curious about things. Especially expensive things. Especially if I'm going to be your wife."

He looked at her without expression.

She said, "Watch the road."

Antonio finally said, "Well I don't know if I want you yet. You promised me you could do three special things to me in my bed that would make me want you, but you overdosed on pasta and were a goner. You sure you want to marry me? You really know what you're getting into?"

Carol said, "I always knew I'd marry someday and you're certainly something in socks. Sure. Life is a dice roll and we'll just hope ours ain't too much in the school of hard knocks. Pull over where nobody can see and I'll show you one of my tricks right now."

"What? Now?"

"You don't need a bed. Believe me."

Antonio smiled like a con. "Can you do it to me now while I'm driving? Is it one of those tricks? I don't want to be late."

"I'll make you crash. You won't take long, I assure you. But park. You'll be so surprised that you won't take long at all."

He smiled big and then pulled down a narrow lane, turned off the engine and parked for six minutes.

* * * * *

Before he was even all they way inside Mama Caltanisseta's door, a nice three room flat, Antonio blurted something in Italian that made her look at Carol in horror and say something back in Italian that didn't sound very happy.

Carol asked, "What'd you say? What'd she say?"

Antonio explained, "That we were going to get married. I told her I needed to get a leg up in life with a real blond on my arm. That is real."

Accompanied by baffling angular gestures, Mama Caltanisseta said to Carol, "Strega! Strega! Strega!"

Carol asked Antonio, "What's that mean?"

"Lovely princess."

"It doesn't sound lovely."

"She's just excited that I'm marrying an Aryan to make me finally a real America, even though I was born in Chicago."

Carol rubbed her hands together greedily. "Well, since your Mama makes spaghetti with black olives in the meatballs, I'm excited too."

Though she was furious, Mama Caltanisseta made tea. When she was finished with her cup, and she saw the pattern that the tealeaves left behind on the bottom, Mama Caltanisseta gasped. She looked in terror at Carol. She grabbed a throw pillow from the couch. Then she went over to Carol and put the pillow in her face and tried to suffocate her."

Antonio was alarmed. "Mama! Mama!" He pulled her away and tossed the pillow even farther.

Carol was stunned. "Why'd she do that?"

Antonio talked to Mama Caltanisseta for a while in Italian until she left the room crying. He said to Carol. "She says she saw in the tealeaves that you killed your first husband by putting a pillow over his face. You now have the mark of the werewolf on your forehead for all to see who have the sight."

"She saw all that on the bottom of her cup?" Carol looked at the bottom of her own. "Huh?" She cautiously touched her forehead. "I'm a werewolf?"

Antonio looked at Carol angrily. "Si. Yes. And she's never wrong."

Carol looked at Antonio angrily. "Have you ever killed

anyone?"

"Plenty."

"Then shut up about it."

Antonio shook his fist at her. "I won't marry a woman who kills husbands! That could make me as nervous as a bag of fleas!"

Carol explained, "He was a crumb. A real rat crumb. He worked in a shoe factory putting together boxes. He drank what little money he made, away. He wouldn't pitch woo with me. Well, he did three times. Three times the first year we were married he gave my any hope that I pleased him. Then he was just of the rest of the time drinking and pretending he was respectable."

"He wouldn't pitch woo with the likes of you? Oh. He was a lowlife cock sucker, that's what he was!"

"A horrible man. A twit. All wet. Horrible. I think I should have a husband like you. Somebody plenty rugged, with a big gun and a big dream. Oh. Wait a minute. After you kill the copper who killed your brother, what are your dreams? Revenge is not really a dream - not a big dream for the future."

"I have very big dreams after I revenge my brother's death. A bunch of us from the family, all us Caltanisseta brothers, we have a plan to take over MGM - and do it in a way so that nobody realizes what we've done until it's too late and we can't be arrested. It'll all look legal. Then we'll live like kings. Do you realize how much dough MGM makes?"

"Why MGM? Why not Republic?"

Antonio shrugged. "I don't know the details. I'm not the brains of this particular operation. I just know the scheme will only work for MGM and for nobody else – for no-place else."

Carol looked sad. "And you'd think I'd be happy since it would make me a star. But if we're going to be married and get rich together, I have to be very honest with you about MGM."

"What. What about it?"

"I heard this through the grapevine telegraph. MGM is going to go bankrupt soon. Just terrible depts. You don't want to take over a business that's all depts."

"What?"

"Have you been paying attention to the films they're releasing?"

Antonio grew nervous. "No. What's that got to do with anything?"

Carol explained, "That's how they make their money. And how they lose it. And MGM made three very expensive pictures to come out at the end of the year and they'll be smarting something terrible after they all flop."

'What pictures."

"Everybody's saying Gone With The Wind is going to be a big flop. Nobody's going to go to it and it cost a fortune. It'll close in a week and it will be the banks that'll declare World War Two, not Hitler."

"That movie is all over in all the press already."

Carol continued, "Sure it is. The studio is spending money it doesn't have to try and get people excited about an old war story, I'm sure. But I read that the director is even so worried about it that he took cash upfront to direct it, instead of waiting for a cut of the profits. He said it would be the biggest white elephant of all time. Because who wants to see a war picture these days with what's going on in Europe? It would just make everybody feel sick."

"And what else is going to flop."

"The Wizard of Oz. It's a mess. It's supposed to be a charming old-fashioned story but they did it all big loud modern art deco. That story has too many fans who don't want to see a story ruined. And Judy Garland is seventeen, now, yet they cast her to play the part of a little girl, anyway. At that age she could have three little girls of her own, by now, if MGM didn't have a pen in the basement they keep her locked up in."

"They really do that?"

Carol nodded earnestly. "I heard it on the streetcar. And they made her silver slippers into red ruby slippers to make the color even more garish. That's MGM."

Antonio scoffed. "Who cares? Nobody will care about that."

"That just shows you're not a movie producer. Like MGM don't seem to have any, anymore. They take the meanings out of everything and for no good reason."

Antonio scratched his head. "Silver has a meaning and ruby doesn't?"

"Yes! The silver slippers going down the road made out of gold bricks were about America expanding its money from just being backed in gold bricks to also being backed in silver, so there could be more money to go around. Then more people, and not just people who are the very richest, can have a shot at having some money. The Wizard of Oz is an American tale about the little people trying to get ahead, but then they just find out that there's no intelligence behind the façade of the big bank building. The big men behind the banks are really humbugs and frauds, like the Wizard. Mama Gravy told me all about it. She is a big fan of the books and she got so mad she screamed when she saw a picture of the red ruby slippers in the movie magazine. She first thought MGM was trying to promote rubies as something to back up currency with. She said MGM was dumber than the banks."

Antonio pointed out, "MGM is not going to make a movie about banks being stupid. Of course they're going to change that part."

Carol felt her blood start to boil. "Well, there's also The Women and that is expected to flop very big! Joan Crawford hasn't had a hit in awhile and so now she got so desperate she's playing a bitch! Her fans won't accept that for a minute! It'll all be all over for her and then MGM will have to pay her a lot of money just to dump her contract. That's what some people think will happen! It's just terrible! It's just awful! I don't know what to do about it! I could just spit!"

Antonio rubbed his face in worry. "It's a shame we can't wait until next year to pull off our scam, but we only have a brief window of time in which to work. Maybe we should just call the whole thing off. I'm plenty worried, now."

"You and me both. Who wants to take over the biggest bankruptcy of all time in the middle of the Great Depression? That's a pretty stupid scam if all you've stolen is a bunch of overdue bills."

"I'll have to hold an emergency meeting with the family. And you better be there to tell them all what you just told me."

Carol smiled. "Sure. Because by then, I'll be family too."

"We don't usually let the dolls into our meetings."

"Get used to it. We're going to be a team. If I'm going to help you find the right copper to plug, then I'm already in as far as you can get. Even before the honeymoon, there'll be blood on our hands."

"Boy, you're a hardboiled egg, aren't you?"

She winked like tough guy, spit in her palm and held it out for him to shake. "Slip me a five. Now take me for a drive in that lovely car. I want to see the sights. I want to see Hollywood! I just gave you good advice and now you're going to pay for it in clovers."

They went along Vine Street to Pinyon Canyon and climbed into it to view an odd land of Spanish houses and Samoan huts and Mediterranean villas and Egyptian, Greek and Oriental Temples, hanging gardens and Islamic gardens, and Tudor cottages, and something out of the Arabian Nights, and a medieval Rhine castle, and a big two story purple pig with windows for eyes. Then they headed west to find Venice Beach to go all the way - to have ice cream with chocolate.

While walking along the glorious stretch of sand, Carol asked all the people who passed her by, "Have you heard of Rita Sunshine's suntan lotion? It smells like coconut cream pie but please don't eat it. It's made using a special electric machine that grinds coffee to dust. Yes, this suntan lotion has coffee in it!"

Nobody had heard of Rita Sunshine. Not one. It made Carol feel sad. She told Antonio all about the ambitious woman who'd given her a lift into town.

* * * * *

Carol walked into The Gold Rush wearing a pretty new dress.

Mama Gravy glared at her. "My. Look at what the cat dragged in. A hairball."

"I'm going to be married."

"Go to Hell. You think you can just come back here like that after snaking off and doing a Garbo? And now you gloat at me and act like you're better than me and give me the high hat like that? How dare you! Who do you think you are? Who do you think I am to care? Go to Hell! Go to Hell and burn and suffer and die and rot and squirm and die and rot and GO TO HELL!"

"I want you to be my bridesmaid."

"Oh?" Mama Gravy was stunned into silence. "What?"

"I want you to be my bridesmaid."

"Oh?"

"Please."

"Really?"

Carol insisted, "Really. You! Smack-bang in the middle of the whole thing. You. You fawning over me."

Mama Gravy said, "And I was going to gloat about how I'd given your bunk away to a better whore. I guess that wouldn't upset you, now, would it? You really getting hitched?"

"Really." Carol begged, "And please say you'll be my bridesmaid. Pleeeeeeeease!"

"Am I the only one you could think to ask? Me?"

Carol nodded. "You're my only best friend in all the world."

"You poor dear." Mama Gravy finally smiled. "Yes. I'd be honored to be somebody's best friend in all the world." Tears started to drop out of her eyes. "I never thought I'd get so far in life as to have something like that at this old age."

Carol looked around. She thought the paper decorations hanging from the ceiling looked like they needed replaced sometime last year, but in the dark nobody paid much attention to what was up above them. "Oh, but you have this fine – fine - business."

"Yes, and I make a few dollars and you all make a few calluses. But once you have something in life, you go on wanting more. You go on wanting what you don't have. Yes I have The Gold Rush. But I didn't have a best friend." She started to bawl. "God bless you dear for asking me to be your bridesmaid. I feel so proud. You have to have the reception here at The Gold Rush. I'll make sure all my girls take a good bath first so all the bachelors have a real good time. There's nothing like a wedding to make people feel good and randy."

"It'll be a small reception at his mother's apartment."

"Who?"

Carol said, "Antonio. And he has a mother."

"That bitch. Oh well, don't worry. I'll wear the prettiest dress. You'll be so proud of me."

They hugged. Carol said, "I'm sure I will."

"And I really didn't give your bunk away. I knew you'd come back. But I just didn't know you'd come back to say something like this. Now I guess I'll have to give your bunk away. I guess now you're gone for good. You went and married the mob. Sweet."

"I don't know if I'd put it that way."

Mama Gravy wagged her finger in Carol's face. "And now that we're best friends and you're married to the mob, I want free dope!"

Carol stammered, "I – I don't know. I don't think I'll have anything to do with that. What do you mean by being married to the mob? I'm just getting married to one man who has a gun, sure, but the mob? That sounds crowded."

"You marry one brother, you might as well marry them all."

Carol was aghast. "They do that in Italy, too? All the brothers want to make whoopee with you?"

"No! Not like that. They don't all go to bed with you. Not on purpose, anyway. I just mean the mob part. You're in their family." Mama Gravy sadly repeated, "I guess now you're gone for good."

"No. Only gone from here as a dancehall hostess. But I'll still come around and we can do other lady things together. Like go to the shops, and things. I don't know. We can even go to the beach and go all the way. What else do ladies do?"

Mama Gravy laughed. "I love chocolate on ice cream! Isn't that outrageous? It's so modern, that's for sure! But other than that, I haven't the slightest idea what ladies do. But I tell you what. You have to take me out, at least, for an engagement party. Your Antonio has to. If I'm going to be your bridesmaid then you have to do that for me. A tit for a tat."

"Where would we take you? A restaurant? The Brown Derby?"

Mama Gravy smiled wickedly. "The Cinderella Bar."

"What kind of bar is that? Why did you smile like you wanted trouble?"

"No trouble. It's just a very unusual place full of twanks, and I want a break from the usual." She looked around wistfully. "For Hollywood, this hootched-up dancehall is outright humdrum. Just a regular Joe."

Carol nodded, "Sure." She wondered what she was getting them all into. "What's a twank?"

"Oh, just some silly slang. You'll see."

* * * * *

At the sight of the building, Carol was ecstatic. "Wooooow. Kippy! And I'm in a new gown. I feel just like the real Cinderella! I am her! I won! I won! "

Mama Gravy looked at Carol in irritation. "Don't be a hayseed. The Cinderella Bar is just a place. Act all aces or you can sit at your own table."

"I'll be keen." She looked down in admiration at her new black satin gown that had been gotten cheap because its cut was about ten years out of date.   She looked back up at the bar and tried not to gasp.

The bar was a stucco building in the shape of a lady's slipper. Carol looked toward her fiancé and Antonio was poker-faced. He grabbed her arm at the door. She thought that was romantic so she smiled up at him.

Antonio explained to her, "So they don't think I'm a fop."

Carol asked, "Why would anybody think that of you? You're pretty rugged."

Mama Gravy laughed and said to Carol, "You'll see."

Antonio added, "This is why Sodom and Gomorrah went up in

flames. To get rid of this."

Mama Gravy laughed. "Well it didn't work, did it. God blew up two cities and mostly just got children and kittens on fire. That's what there is most of in any city. Oh, and rats. God got himself a lot of rats that day."

Carol asked, "I don't understand. What is that story about? Did God really blow up two cities to get rid of the rats?" They were in the door. "How is this like Sodom and Gomorrah?"

Mama Gravy urgently shushed her.

Inside, there was a place for a floorshow and there were small round tables. They were led to one and they ordered champagne.

Antonio said, "That was expensive."

Mama Gravy waved the waiter off. "You're paying for the entertainment, also. Wait until you see the show this place puts on." She laughed.

Carol asked again, "Tell me about the story of Sodom and Gomorrah. I've always wanted to know."

Antonia said, "God blows up sinners. Rains down fire from Heaven."

Carol frowned and sadly touched the top of her head. "Fire?" She suddenly didn't want to hear any more. "Let's talk about me."

A blonde woman in a man's sporting jacket walked by their table. Mama Gravy grabbed her arm and blurted, "What's Francis Farmer sculling around here for?"

Francis looked down at her in irritation. "What." She raised her thickly drawn-on black kohl eyebrows in utter disdain.

Mama Gravy said, "I didn't know you were a homosexual."

"Fuck me and the baby's yours!" Francis laughed and sat down. She was clearly drunk. She tipped what was left of their bottle down her throat, and then said, "Honey. I ain't Sapphic."

"The way you're dressed. You in the act?"

Carol finally found her voice. "You. You? You're Francis Farmer?"

Francis replied, "I look just like her, don't I?" Then she said to Mama Gravy, "No, I don't clown for anybody. I just dressed like this tonight because I felt like it. I say fuck gender."

Mama Gravy raised her empty glass. "Alleluia to that."

Francis Farmer regarded Antonio. "I wouldn't put you in a dress. You look just fine the way you are." She winked.

He smiled, charmed, and to reward her he ordered another bottle of champagne and an extra glass.

Carol felt like she'd suddenly lose her chance at marriage. So she announced why they were there.

Francis Farmer said, "Well three cheers and a tiger! But, hey. If this is a bridal party, then why is there a fellah here?" She grabbed Antonio's arm.

Mama Gravy said, "Somebody's gotta pony up."

Francis Farmer licked her lips. "Sweet. I sure ain't. I'm flat broke." She laughed. "And drunk just the same. That's the only good part about being a movie star. You can be way in dept and still run around in booze and new shoes!"

Carol marveled, "I just love you! You're just so fantastic. You're just such a fantastic star!"

Francis looked upon Carol and said, "My aren't you just as funny as a piece of string."

"Really! Truly. Really and truly!"

"Put your eyeballs back in your head." Francis added, "Nobody wants to be drooled over."

Carol blurted, "I just loved you in Ride a Crooked Mile. You were so beautiful."

"I was shit. It was shit. Paramount is shit. The horse gave a shit. This town is horseshit. This is good booze. If I had an ulcer, I think it just ate it away."

Carol repeated, "You were so beautiful up there on the big screen like that. You're the biggest star!"

Francis said, "Well, you know what the big fish said to the little fish at the farm pond."

Carol guessed, "I'm going to eat you?"

"Pond scum rises to the top. It don't matter if you're not pond scum when you first show up, but the pond will transform you in no time into pure Hollywood sparkly pond scum."

"Pond scum?" Carol was confused, so she repeated, "But you're so beautiful up on the big screen!"

"They made me look like a clown. I'm in the Wild West with false eyelashes? And everything else plucked to shit? Everything was so humbug. I tried to reason with them but they just wanted to talk about how they were going to light me so that when the men in the audience sees me they all ejaculate at the exact same time."

Mama Gravy winked at her. "And some of us ladies, too."

Carol asked of Francis' present appearance, "Why did you draw your eyebrows so big?"

"Fuck them. They pluck all our faces off so we all leave Makeup looking all the exact same. They won't let you be an individual in Hollywood. I told them leave my goddam eyebrows alone - they're mine you fuckers you lousy fuckers. I tried to stop them and they threatened to strap me down to my chair. Fuck them. Fuck them! Who are they to pluck my face off? They don't own me that way. They think they do. They think they have my soul in a little jar locked in the producer's office. But they don't. Fuck them, I say. Goddamit! Shit! Fuck! A little more of this booze, please. Be a dear."

Carol asked excitedly. "You're doing a picture now?"

"No. And they still pluck and pluck like I'm a dead chicken. They said I had to still pluck everything pluckable for publicity shots. I said if it's just publicity shots you want, and studio shots at that, then paint the eyebrows out, later, if you want. Paint my nose out for all I care. Take an old tossed-off picture of Marlene Dietrich and repaint it and say it's me, for all I care. They make us all look the same, anyway. What's the difference? Does anybody even know what Marlene Dietrich really looks like behind all that getup? That's all Hollywood issues out. Regulation detail Marlene eyebrows for everybody."

Mama Gravy said, "Carol wants to be a star."

"What shit. There goes your face." Francis looked at Carol's hairline. "It looks like it could be plucked a bit more. They'll keep you in that makeup chair until you look as bland as a bar of soap."

Carol seemed hurt. "Why?"

"Oh fuck it all." Then Francis Farmer's expression got devilish. "But I can say with some charity - that there's really nothing wrong with this town that a few good films can't fix."

Carol said, "Films are fun! Some of them."

"Chewing gum for the eyes."

Carol was astonished.

"Ah, save it. A trip to Hollywood is a trip for biscuits. Sure you can make a bundle. They throw money at you like it's nothing. But then they make sure they hold you down and stomp on your face for it, before you can go!"

Mama Gravy gave Francis a big nudge to lighten her up. "A real comedy cyclone."

Francis said, "Hollywood has got to be seen to be disbelieved."

"Aw," Carol pouted. "You're such a big star. You made it to the top. Can't you say anything nice about being such a Hollywood goddess?"

Francis pretended to grow kind. "Hmmm. God finally felt sorry for actors so He gave them someplace with swimming pools. He's a real sport."

Mama Gravy nudged Francis again, this time gently. "I thought you was an atheist."

Francis loudly laughed at herself.

Carol said, "Mama Gravy, here, told me once that you'd go down in history as the biggest star of the forties."

Francis sneered. "I don't want it. I want to be a real actress and support my theatre group in New York and get back there as soon as I can. That's real art. We're trying to be real. Wake the audience up from its daydream! See the world for what it really is! This shit here is all glitter and mist. And fake smiles. And goddam tap dancing for no reason. Junk. They said they needed great new ammo and I was their star bullet. Pow! Right in the brain! Me!"

Carol was puzzled. "Then why did you come here and become such a beautiful star?"

"To make a big fat wad of money - money to send to New York to the Group Theatre. They're all I care about. If it wasn't for these slave plantation contracts, I'd be there right now. But this is America, land of the free. Free bullshit. You're only free until you need to make some money to eat. Then suddenly the freedom belongs to your slave master. Bullshit!"

Mama Gravy said, "I'm never wrong. I bet your work with the New York group will help make you famous world over like no other star has been. And then you'll take Bette Davis' parts away from her. And she'll disappear for all time. Mark my words. I'm never wrong. You'll last. You got talent and beauty!"

"You're all full of shit. You need to learn to see. See that you're a slave. See that you're ridiculous. See that you're all in just some damn slapstick sideshow you call your life. It's time to get serious before it's too late. Thanks for the booze. Thanks for kissing my ass." Francis got up, a bit unsteadily, and then staggered to the steps. She walked up them sideways more than forward, to keep her balance.

Carol said, "Wow!" Then she glanced back to the steps. "Oh my god!"

Francis was upside-down. She had fallen on her back, with her heels at the top step. Six waiters ran to her, lifted her up off the steps and then pushed her out the door.

Mama Gravy yelled out. "Ooopsi daisy!"

Antonio asked, "Do you think she may have hurt her head?"

Mama Gravy waved him off. "Don't be such a perfect gentleman. If she cracked her head open at this point in her evening, only a bit of mud would come out."

After a moment of reflective silence, Carol finally marveled, "I just talked to a real live star."

Mama Carol scoffed. "Oh, she was a rude cow. It's a shame that it's the rude ones that get famous."

Carol asked, Antonio, "What did you think of her? Wasn't it swell? Wasn't it swell to celebrate our engagement with a real live star?"

Antonio said with great certainty, "She has slipped off her trolley.

Insane."

Mama Gravy laughed to blissfully agree.

Carol didn't care. "She was still a star. Francis Farmer. She's up and coming, still, and will be the greatest star of all time, I bet. We were with real Hollywood royalty. And she sat and talked to us like we were somebodys. I'll always treasure this night. I'll always remember it as the special Francis Farmer night." She turned to Antonio and a tear fell from her eye. "Thank you, honey. Thank you for taking us ladies out on the town." Then she jolted. "Oh my!" She angrily slapped her leg.

"What?" Antonio asked in alarm.

"I forgot to ask her for her autograph."

Antonio was relieved. "The way said oh my, it was like you'd lost your purse, or something."

"Getting an autograph is important."

Mama Gravy said, "Don't be a hayseed. She wouldn't have done it anyway. She's not that kind of star to give autographs. She's rude."

Antonio repeated, "And insane."

Then a man dressed up like he thought he was Marlene Dietrich walked up to the edge of the stage in a wild-west saloon dress and held two water guns. In a low husky voice, he said, "Mawana moo wah wah woo woo ha."

Mama Gravy said, "Speaking of the devil. Look. Francis Farmer's twin sister in eyebrows." She yelled up to the stage, "That western you just made is gonna flop."

He made an angry pose with his guns. "Wowanah woo wannah bah wainah."

Mama gravy added, "And learn English while you're at it, or are you talking like that again because you forgot to rinse your sauerkraut!"

"Wanna woo Mawanah." He turned on his heel and left.

Carol asked, "What was he saying? Why was he doing that? He sounded awful."

Mama Gravy explained, "Sounded just like her. Brilliant! That was a brilliant impersonation!"

A man dressed up like Cleopatra stepped out onto the stage, and yelled off to where there weren't even any people. "I'm not Theda Bera, you bitch. I'm Claudette Colbert. I'm rich. And now for our show tonight, we ain't gonna have one." He looked at Carol's table. "There ain't enough people to bother. Maybe at midnight we'll try something if we've had enough to drink." He walked off.

"Rude!" Mama Gravy yelled.

Chapter Eight

Walking down the block from the car to the church where Carol would receive Catholic instruction before she'd be married, she noticed the hats people were wearing. Several men who weren't cowboys wore cowboy hats. And there were wanna-be mountaineers, sea captains, yachters, and baseball players. She was amused, and said aloud to them all, "Only in Hollywood."

"What?" Antonio asked, who was with her to meet the priest. He hadn't been in a church since Chicago.

"Oh nothing."

Next to the church was an MGM movie theater. A poster in front advertised Laurence Olivier in Wuthering Heights. Carol paused long enough to imagine her image painted in his arms. "I need to use more elbow grease if I'm going to be up there and not down here."

Antonio asked, "What?"

"I'm going to be a star."

"I thought you were going to be a Catholic so you can be my wife."

"That too. I want it all"

The priest found Carol a quick student. She was thrilled to find she could memorize things easily - that would come in handy for scripts. The process of becoming a Catholic was finally hastened even faster when Carol suddenly had the memory of already being a Catholic. As a little girl she went to a country church, St. Mary's, with a fascinating Madonna statue in a cave-like hollow fashioned above the front doors. The doors were painted a rich blue. And there was a small picturesque cemetery plot just spitting distance behind it that her brothers used to tell her terrifying stories about, so that during many of the services she was filled with great fear of crawling bones coming down the isle for her. She didn't even get to the wee age of receiving first communion yet. The family had stopped going when her mother had been gored by the bull and died. The memory of it all was now like slow motion grainy movies shot in 16mm belonging to somebody else and she had just happened to see them once from a distance, from another house, through a window of dusty gingham curtains and wavy glass.

"But I remember it all, now."

* * * * *

At the church basement, Mama Gravy helped Carol get dressed. As Carol's veil was being arranged, she looked down at the top of her head and said, "This covers where your hair was all burned off pretty good. It's a miracle it's growing back finally."

"Finally."

"Give it a year to be back where it was."

Carol asked, "How did you get your name? We talked about it a little a long time ago but it made you sad. Why?"

"Who cares?"

"You're my only and best friend and I don't know you very well."

Mama Gravy said, "I told you I went to college for a year to be a teacher - that I even thought about being a nun so I could teach in a Catholic school. I even told you a nun joke. You know more than most."

Carol prodded her. "Come on. I want to know more. Your name is unusual."

Mama Gravy was flattered. "You do care, don't you. Mitt me kid. Most people don't even really see you unless you're rich. Okay, so I'll tell you. I had a friend in college and we shared the same bed. You know what I mean. A very special lady friend."

"Sure. A college homosexual lover."

Mama Gravy smiled sadly. "She was the one who talked most about us becoming nuns so we could teach at a really nice school. But she didn't look much like a nun. Sure, she wore the penguin colors, but it was top hat and tails for her. She loved to walk around in like she was famous. She called me Mama because she said I was her Mama. And she said I was like gravy on everything because I made everything better. And then one day she put them together and called me Mama Gravy and it stuck. We were together all the time and it was like we were the same person. I was the right arm and she was the left arm of somebody bigger than us. We were the arms of God. Aaaaah. Those were the days."

"What happened to her? Did she become a nun?"

"No. Some mean drunk men pushed her under a trolley and she was cut into three pieces. Those horrible men!"

Carol asked, "Did they go to prison?"

"No. They ran off and we didn't know where to go and find them."

"That's terrible! So you decided not to be a nun at all? You know - you can be a nun and not have anything to do with children, if you don't like them much."

Mama Gravy frowned. "I don't want to talk about all that. Let's just say it wasn't in the cards for me. My life went someplace else after the horrible shock of that. My life - " she sadly faded off.

"So what's your real name?"

"Like yours, my new name is now my real name. In this town, everything is made-up, even the people. That's why we come here – to make ourselves up so that we can finally have something to live with."

Carol asked, "How did you know my name is made up?"

"It's Hollywood. It's safe to assume so, if you want to be right. What's your real name?"

Carol bargained, "I'll tell you mine if you tell me yours."

"Sure."

"I'm really Karin Panotchitch. Or was. I ain't going back."

Mama Gravy gasped. "Oh, my. That name was a bit of heavy weather."

"Karin with a K."

"Ouch. That's not very movie star - and so German. They're not very popular these days, not the fashion, not with Hitler making trouble. You made a good change."

"What's yours?"

"Helen Grace."

"That sounds so pretty."

"I don't want to sound pretty. I run a cathouse and I'm a dirty sinner. Mama Gravy seems to suit me better. Helen Grace – what a pushover. Anybody named Helen Grace would get robbed three times a day."

Carol pondered. "Now I'll have an Italian name. Will that keep me from being a star?"

"You gotta keep your old name. Pan is a star name. Not Caltanisseta."

"Sure. But let's not tell Mr. husband about it for a while." She held her veil out. "Boy do I look kippy. Just aces." She pinched her cheeks.

"Pretty as you can be. This dress cost Antonio a lot, didn't it?"

Carol nodded excitedly. "It's used, sure. And a little old fashioned. But I'm not poor anymore. Am I? Not like I was. In fact I'm eating meatballs every night! Pinch me!"

"No, you ain't no poor girl no more. Now you're a lady. The real kind. While your husband is out working hard rat-a-tatting new ventilation holes in the city – playing big guy with his Tommy gun - you'll be under some marvelous chandelier eating caviar and chocolates and donuts filled with whatever you want."

Carol frowned. "Don't say it like that. You make it sound so naughty. And we ain't rich, yet. He says he has some deals to go through, and since the plan to take over MGM is off, it'll take a lot longer to make it. What a shame MGM hadn't planned on making some good movies this year, that's for sure."

Mama Gravy squeezed her shoulder. "We really saved him there, didn't we kid?"

"Yes. He'll always be grateful. After The Wizard of Oz and Gone With the Wind flop my husband and his brothers will be kissing our feet for having warned them. But I hope maybe next year then he gets a chance to muscle in on a motion picture studio, however one does that. And I don't think you run in with guns blazing. I think it has something to do with a lawyer and tax evasion and dead bodies planted around to embarrass people – or whatever it was I heard the brothers saying at Mama Caltanisseta's. Oh, and I also heard them say you have to put heroin in some people's cars and then call the cops on them, and then make sure the dead bodies are found next. That's it. And then somebody they've code named Agent X is found at the bottom of somebody's swimming pool. I didn't hear it all but business deals get complicated and this one need some breathing room I guess. You need to plan on times when you just have to think on your feet."

Mama Gravy groaned. "That sounds all cockamamie to me. But maybe those brothers are on to something. Really. Wouldn't that just be something? Maybe you really can hijack a whole studio and make it look like nobody blinked. They do that to the White House and that other big organization, the CCCDC, all the time, and only about three people bother barking."

"What's the CCCCCD?"

"CCCDC! The Chamber of Commerce Christmas Decorating Committee, of course. Don't you pay attention to the lights on Hollywood Boulevard or haven't you been here long enough yet?"

"No, and yes, everything is always being taken over by everybody else, isn't it? I just want it to happen someday at a studio so Antonio can make me a star! Like Norma Shearer has Irving Thalberg to make her look good. He's been giving her all the plum roles at MGM since they married."

Mama Gravy chortled. "What a gold digger. Well if you can't do a Norma, and marry a production executive, then, hey, marry the guy who's gonna plug him full of holes."

"Amen!" Carol folded her hands and said a nervous prayer, "Let me be married a long long time full of happiness and if anything bad happens I blame you. I know you're tricky – you made Hitler be born and invented the Japanese, but please, don't play games with me. Hail Mary, full of grace, and hopefully a lot of favors for me and a lot of baby boys. Amen." She stood up from the mirror and they both fluffed her skirts.

"A lot of baby boys to hand down all those Tommy Guns to."

Carol said, "Hey, you make it all sound so terrible. And in a church with Mama Caltanisseta upstairs waiting for her cut of whatever her sons make, the greedy witch. But I got to pretend to like her since we eat her home cooking every night. I got to be nice since I sure can't cook that way. And boy is it good! So I gotta like her at least until I learn how."

Mama Gravy kissed her cheek. "That's like having to kiss an alligator."

Carol shrugged. "She gives me the evil eye, sure, but she cooks real good. Now you tell me which one is more important – her nasty peepers or my happy stomach? But she always has tomato salad and grapes and things like that. Isn't that kind of food isn't healthy, is it? It's all water, right?"

Mama Gravy nodded. "Those Italians are crazy about their vegetables, and I agree. It's a waste of time to eat all that water."

Somebody shouted down the staircase at them to ask if they were ready.

"Coming!" Mama Gravy yelled back up.

"Yes. There. I think I'm ready. Now let's go upstairs and get me hitched to a man that's gonna make sure my ship comes in."

* * * * *

As prepared as Carol thought she was for a wedding mass, starring her, nobody warned her that she wouldn't know what was being said. It was in Latin. It left her feeling like she was in a foreign film. She'd never seen one before and decided she never would. She kept glancing over to Mama Gravy who wouldn't stop looking around at all the statues. Carol looked at the statue of the Virgin Mary, regarding her finely painted eyebrows.

After communion, as the newlyweds were getting up from their a kneeling position, they heard a rumble, then a sick crunching sound, then all the statues wobbled dangerously. Before Carol could decide what door she might race out of in a wedding gown that would want to trip her up, the trembling stopped. The statues settled. Nothing fell but a bit of dust over the baptistery. Carol decided that not getting squashed was a good luck sign. Mama Caltanisseta decided the earthquake was a bad sign but it was too late for her opinion. I do had been said.

At the door, just before the new couple would run outside into the rice gauntlet, Carol asked Mama Gravy, "These earthquakes happen all the time?"

She made a worried face, tensely baring her teeth. "Not that big."

Carol was surprised. "That was big? The one in San Francisco with Jeanette MacDonald was much bigger. What didn't all fall down was later all blown up, to keep fire from spreading all over the whole city."

"Count your blessings. You didn't get hit in the head with a brick."

"Yes. I have blessings now. I'm now a bride."

As Mama Caltanisseta threw rice at Carol like she wanted to hurt her, a pigeon flying overhead pooped his chalky slop on Carol's veil crown and nose. Carol looked to Mama Gravy as if it was her fault for allowing it, being the bridesmaid. Mama Gravy laughed hysterically. Mama Caltanisseta gasped in surprise.

Antonio said something in Italian at his mother, and then he told Carol, "In Italy it's good luck to be pooped on by a bird. My Mama isn't sure yet that she wants you to have good luck."

"Good luck!" Carol exclaimed, "I'm finally going to have good luck!" She turned to Mama Gravy and said, "Maybe I really will become a star!"

Mama Gravy replied, "You'd have a better chance of getting pooped on by the same bird every Wednesday for a month. In December."

* * * * *

At the reception afterwards at Mama Caltanisseta's, the first thing to make her convinced that tragedy would befall the family was to step in the door and see her picture of Mary crooked. Antonio tried to explain to his Mama that such a thing was good luck after an earthquake. That it could have been much worse. She only calmed after she ate some of her own delicious meatballs.

Antonio offered her, "Have some zucchini."

Carol put up her hand. "A waste of chewing. Vegetables are mostly water and no protein."

"Italian food is good. Vegetables are good."

"Yes, dear, whatever you say." Carol saw a cockroach on a Chippendale style curio shelf. The bug reminded her of when she lived in that dank one-room basement apartment with her first husband. She remembered how on some days a few bugs were all she had to eat. She wondered if she should make a great display of eating this one to show them all the thin line between starving and sipping champagne. She decided against it. It would require too much of an explanation. So Carol got up and discretely squashed it with her finger and rolled it in her napkin. The mother-in-law who should thank her was doing her best to always keep her back to her, even though her daughter-in-law had been so blessed with an unexpected anointment from the Heavens of bird poop.

Mama Gravy said, "Boy that earthquake had me thinking I was going to lose a few feet off my height, being inside such a big old' building like that. Squash!"

Carol nodded. "I wonder what makes the earth to shake in some places, like Hollywood?"

Mama Gravy explained, "I learned about it in school. Did you know earth is cooling and as it does it's wrinkling and that causes earthquakes. That's what the scientists believe."

"Oh my." After Carol finished her tea, Mama Caltanisseta grabbed the cup and looked inside at the small soggy black lump of leaves She told Antonio something.

Carol asked him, "What did she say to you?"

"You would travel abroad your life, but not your feet."

Carol looked at her new husband in surprise. "You're taking me to Italy without my feet? Who chops off my feet? Why would anyone want to do something like that?"

Antonio said, "I was not in the vision. And don't worry about your feet. It's all poetry, I'm sure."

"That's odd. You must be in the vision. We'll be together forever. It's a Catholic marriage. Forever and ever and ever."

Antonio corrected her. "We'll be together until one of us dies."

Mama Gravy said, "Let's not talk about such things as death like this at a time like this. I think it's probably bad luck to speak of it. Oh, and in school they said the earth is going to cool and cool until it's such a prune that someday we're all going to fall into the deep valleys and be crushed into dust."

Mama Caltanisseta began to wail, "Morte! Morte!" until one of the other brothers, Fredrico, brought her more of her savory breaded zucchini.

* * * * *

The first thing Antonio said, after they woke up in his barren apartment on Sunset Boulevard was, "Let's go find the stinking copper who plugged my brother."

Carol opened her eyes. "Today?"

"Now."

"What about our honeymoon?"

Antonio smiled like a con. "I'll be making whoopee when I get back. For my brother. For me. For the world."

"What? I'd rather it just be for you."

They dressed and got in his car. Carol asked, "Now how much does this car cost? It's so fine."

"I won it in Chicago. A gambling win. Pretty sweet, huh."

"Was it won fair and square?"

"You bet." He winked at her. "And then he found himself at the bottom of the river."

"You serious?" Carol gasped. "You actually killed somebody for their car? That's rude!"

"Just kidding. Gosh you're a hayseed this morning."

"I'm nervous." Carol admitted. "What if the copper doesn't like being shot at? What if he shoots you first?"

Antonio pulled out a pistol. "This baby is the finest thing made. She won't fail me."

"What if the copper ain't out on the street today?"

Antonio said, "Then I'll have my revenge tomorrow. Or the day after that. We'll drive around where you last saw him until you see him again. All you have to do, dollface, is point that pretty little ring finger at him."

* * * * *

They drove off. So that Antonio would be free to shoot while they were on the move, Carol offered to drive. She drove all over the place.

"Not that side of the road!"

Carol said, "But there's nobody else on it and I want to turn up there."

"There will be and go slower on the turns or you'll miss them!"

"But your car goes so fast! Weeeee!"

"Stop the car!"

Carol asked, "Right here?"

"No! Not in that lane! Stop it over there where it belongs!" She stopped the car very abruptly. He yelled, "Not here! I thought you said you could drive a car."

"Well, sure. Away I went." She hit the gas and put them in a yard. "Ooops."

Antonio yelled, "Don't you know where a car goes? Don't you know what lane to ever drive in! Or what a stop sign is!"

"Well, I did learn to drive growing up on my neighbor's tractor. There are no confusing lanes in a field."

Antonio said, "So you don't know how to drive!"

Carol reminisced, "I knew that if I could drive that tractor, that was so hard to steer and shift, with a clutch like the devil, then I could drive anything. This car drives like a breeze."

"Yeah, palsy, as you breeze us both right over a cliff. I drive. You point him out. I'll stop the car and get out and shoot him dead. Don't do anything but sit real nice in the passenger's seat and be a doll."

"Okay. Calm down. You're going to have a heart attack."

* * * * *

They drove around for three days. They kept passing a wild man in a crosswalk. He was yelling about how they needed to repent or God would burn the city down because they were all such sinners. And the car radio kept talking about Hitler.

Carol finally turned the radio off and said, "I'm tired of that – that Hitler."

Antonio said, "At the drugstore they said the right wing conservatives in our own government are the ones really wanting to go back to war. That's how they live. War. The last World War left so much undone and the conservatives didn't want to fix any of it with treaties and international clubs. They wouldn't support any efforts to stop Hitler years ago. They just want war."

"Is that all you men talk about? War, war, war, fiddle-dee-dee, as Miss Scarlet would say. Now how do I turn you off like a radio? I'm tired of all this talk of war. It makes me nervous. The sky is falling, the sky is falling, boo hoo."

Antonio said, "On the radio, you'll never hear the conservatives blamed for anything. They own the radio."

Carol said, "I didn't know you were such a Red."

"I ain't and you know it. When you're a Red you can't make a fast buck. Call me a Red now and I'll laugh in your face. Call me a Red after I get poisonously rich and everybody else will laugh in your face. All the Reds want to do is share what little there is with a whole crowd of bozos you don't even know, and wouldn't want to. I'll have it the other way around, thank you. But that doesn't mean I want war. But I guess it's too late now. There has to be war. You can't take Hitler back."

"Fiddle-dee-dee."

* * * * *

Then, just to be over with it, as they were driving around aimlessly for the third day in a row, Carol felt lazy and finally pointed out any old copper she saw. "That's him. He lost some weight but I'm sure of it."

"Let's do him in." Antonio stopped the car so fast it was Carol's turn to go into the dashboard. He ran to the copper, pulled out his pistol and squeezed the trigger. Nothing happened. The copper pulled out his gun and shot Antonio full of holes.

Carol slid behind the wheel and drove away. She heard the copper yell, "Wait!"

"Oh crap. I bet he even got my license plate number. Oh no. What do I do? What do I do? What do I do?" She tried to drive correctly through her tears.

"Watch it lady! Those are tulips under there!"

"Hey lady! That's a stop sign!"

"Lady! That's not a road!"

She dried her eyes so she could see. By now she had the city pretty memorized. Careful to not take the corner too fast, and to stay in the correct lane, she pulled into a used car lot that she'd seen dozens of times. She tried to look as serious as she could to the man who came out to her. Through new tears, she said, "This car isn't very nice. Is it?"

"Sure, lady?"

"I mean - for a lady like me. I don't know what I want. Could I sell this to you for cash today? How much is it worth?"

"Cash? You think we just have a room full of stacks of dough here?"

Carol thought fast. "Or - or a money order. I suppose all the cash is in the bank, isn't it."

He nodded.

Carol asked again, "How much is this car worth? What is it, even?"

"It's a 1937 De Soto Coupe. New, it was worth eighth hundred and twenty dollars. Used, I don't now. I'd have to look it over, and look in the book to see how far it's depreciated in the last few years. This your car? Can you prove it?"

Carol let out a gasp of grief. "It was my husband's car. My husband is dead. It was his most expensive possession. I'm afraid I really need the cash. Or a money order. Or a bank check. Please!"

"Are you sure?"

"I can't eat a car!"

The man went to the glove compartment and pulled out papers. "Here they are. That's all I need. It goes against the book but you have an honest face. And my wife has pointed out to me many times how a wife doesn't have rights. She don't get her own bank account and things. I understand how hard it is for a lady to get those things in order when her husband dies. You have my full sympathy. I'll give you half of it's original worth."

"Half? That's not a good deal."

"Half or leave it."

Carol wanted to bawl again. "Half?"

"I'm sticking my neck out, here. Half or nothing."

"Okie-doke. Let me just check the trunk, first." Carol peeked in the trunk to find nothing but a spare tire and jack. "Oh good." She took a bank check and walked to Wurdenbocker and Romrig Federal Savings and Trust.

* * * * *

It took until evening for Carol to get to Antonio's brother, Fredrico's apartment. "He's dead!" She blurted. Dead, dead, dead!"

"Who?"

"Antonio!"

Fredrico jumped up. "How?"

"He wanted to kill the copper! The copper killed him! Shot

him dead!"

"That fool! How could he have been such a fool? He was supposed to be the brains. What a fool? Now what are we going to do? He'd said he had a new plan to make some money? Did he tell you what he was thinking? What were his plans?"

Carol was confused. "He did? He told me somebody else was the brains."

"No. He was."

"That's not what he told me."

Fredrico said, "I know what I'm talking about. You're just a dame. Don't question me. Now the brains are dead."

"He's dead! He's dead!"

"We'll all be dead in the street if he don't get our heads screwed back on."

Carol nodded. "I know. I'm just so upset. I was planning on a married life."

Fredrico said, "Now we just have to screw our heads on."

"Can I spend the night here? I can't go back there right now."

"Sure. I'll sleep on the couch."

Carol asked, "When did you last change your sheets?"

"I don't know, why?"

"I'll sleep on your couch."

* * * * *

At breakfast, Carol proposed to Fredrico, "Maybe we can rob a bank."

"What?"

Carol nodded urgently. "Rob a bank."

Fredrico said, "That's just dollars to donuts."

"What?"

"Too risky. The odds are too long."

"Naw, I know a screenwriter who wrote a story about it. I can read his screenplay and learn how they did it and copy his plan."

"Don't be a dope. I bet the story ends with them all getting shot in the end. After what the Barker Gang got away with, they're more careful at banks, now."

Carol said, "Well, that's where the money is."

Fredrico said, "That's why it's too obvious. We need to kidnap somebody. That way the money comes to us."

Carol said, "Isn't that illegal? No matter what you do, you got this person in the way - you're still left standing somewhere with your pants down and you're holding the bag."

"Don't' be a dope."

"Robbing a bank seems more like getting to the point, if you're going to commit a crime. And kidnapping reminds me of that awful thing that happened to that poor baby."

Fredrico said, "I mean we'll do it in a bigger way since the Lindberg baby. I agree. That was horrible. I'd never do that. No babies. We'll only kidnap a full grown man that somebody wants to pay for so it ain't so bad."

Carol said, "Well, if we do a kidnapping, we'll need to take some wet sock who deserves it. But somebody that we know for sure has somebody who will pay to get him back."

"A nazi?"

Carol gave him an impatient glare. "Who would pay to get a stupid Nazi back?"

Fredrico explained, "Other Nazis? There a whole group of them here in town who write the American Protestant newspaper."

"Oh, sure. I read all about them. It's just a sideshow."

Fredrico waved his hand before his nose. "And they stink. Those guys make me sore. They say horrible things about Catholics."

"And they have Nazi meetings. I read all about it once in my Look Magazine. So I know all about it all. The editor lives right in West Hollwood He's the Reverend Blanche. He even writes books. They're all about how his religion is better than the Catholics."

Fredrico smiled. "A reverend? Hmmm. I'm sure many will pay to see him back. He should just be dropped off a cliff - but a dead man ain't worth nothing."

"We'll need disguises, won't we?"

Fredrico nodded. "First we need a plan."

"And that starts with how I'm going to look. When you make plans with a lady you always start with how she's going to look."

Chapter Nine

Fredrico's disguise was in place. He wore a stolen copper outfit, a fake moustache that didn't look too phony in the shade, and sunglasses. After he was suitably dappered-up, he went to find out who the Reverend Blanche was. He went to where the American Protestant was published.

There was a big sign on the wall. It read,

Make America Fascist. Make America Strong:

1) War against all enemies without and within, large and small
2) Strengthen nationalism, heighten allegiance to the President.
3) Crush organized labor, protect business
4) Control elections, control courts, control airwaves
5) Put God back into science and the arts, censor intellectuals
6) Put God back into government (Protestant naturally)
7) Stop the women's vote, increase the birth rate
8) Put the simpletons back in their place working the cotton fields
9) Put all criminals to death, find more criminals
10) Stop immigration. Increase deportation (whites exempt).

"May we help you, officer?"

Fredrico hollered imposingly, in a cute Irish accent, "Mr. Blanche. I am here to see Mr. Blanche."

A man in black clothes stepped forward. "Reverend. And what do you want from me, sir?"

"Your car is parked funny and it's been getting complaints. Come out now and re-park it."

The Reverent Blanche ordered somebody else, "Johnny. Go re-park my car. If it really needs it. I think the Irishman has just had too much to drink so far today."

Fredrico yelled, "No. You re-park your own car. To teach you a lesson about parking it right in the first place. I don't want to ever have to come back and talk to you about this again."

The Reverend Blanche grumbled and grabbed his keys. "I can smell your gorilla hair from here."

"What did you say?"

"Oh. Nothing. I was just talking to Johnny. He spelled something wrong."

"Hurry."

As the man re-parked his car, which was parked just fine in the first place, Fredrico watched. Then he went to his own car, and said to Carol, "Now I know who he is and what car he drives."

Carol was in her disguise. Wearing no lip rouge or eye paint, which she hadn't gone without in a long time, now, made her seem like she had a much tinier face. Her skin was temporarily ruined by moles. They were made out of rubbed-down pencil erasers painted sable and glued on with spirit gum. All of her hair was up under a tight headscarf. She said, "Now we wait and I hope he don't work late."

Carol asked, "What did all you brothers do in Chicago? Was it fun? I hear there's lots of mob there. It must have been fun for you."

"Yeah, it's a good place for an Italian."

She made sure her hair was still all under her scarf, and then situated her dress. "We better make a lot of money off of all this hard work."

"What are we going to do with you?"

"What do you mean? Do with me? I'm right here."

"I mean long term. My brother is dead. We just can't leave a pretty thing like you being a widow for the next fifty years."

"Pretty! In this disguise? I hope we get him before my moles pop off. I'm bored waiting like this. Working is supposed to be work."

"You know what I mean. You're pretty and you know it. Let me play with your knobbers for awhile to pass the time."

"No way!" She put her arms up over her bra. "Don't you dare!"

"Why not? Don't be shy. It's just knobbers and you ain't married anymore."

"No way!"

Fredrico squeezed at the air. "It'll help pass the time."

"You try and touch me up here and I'll run away. You got it? I'll run. And fast. I'll make like a squirrel and scram!"

"You have a hang up with your body?"

"Just keep your hands down."

"Whatever. I can see now they don't look real, anyway. All lumps. What did you pad them with? Parking tickets?"

"Sure. Parking tickets. And I don't want you bothering them."

Fredrico teased her: "You'll never be a star with knobbers stuffed like that."

"I want to be a star!"

"You say that like you almost forgot."

Carol frowned. "Well it's hard to keep myself on track. It's hard to always think about being a star when there's so much other stuff going on. Like living. But I want to be a star."

"You've tried everything?"

Carol nodded. "That I can think of. I even set myself on fire to be a star, and it's hard to top that. I don't know what else to do."

Fredrico asked, "Have you tried selling your soul to the Devil?"

"No. Does it work?"

"It depends."

"How."

Fredrico explained, "You have to go to an unmarked crossroads in the desert. At midnight he will come, if you call him. Then you name your desires – then he names his price. Your soul."

"That all?"

Fredrico said, "You have to be brave enough to do it. You have to be sorry enough to want to give up your own soul."

"I ain't afraid of no Devil. If he was so scary then everybody would always be running around screaming bloody hell. The only thing to be afraid of these days is the Germans and the Japs and Italy.

They're doing worse than taking souls. They're taking lives!"

Fredrico said, "Leave Italy out of our conversations."

Carol asked, "What if I go all the way out to the desert and find a crossroads and it's midnight and no Devil shows up. That's what will happen, and it'll happen because you've set me up for a practical joke."

"No," Fredrico said, "If you do that, and no Devil shows up, it'll be because you already are a bad girl. The Devil would never show up to take the soul of somebody who's already lost it. He only wants good girl's souls that he don't already have."

"Serious?"

"That's what they say in Sicily. And they don't lie there. They can't afford to. They can't afford anything in Sicily. So the good things in life have to be free."

Carol quickly put her hands over her bra.

* * * * *

At five on the dot, the Reverend Blanche was out the door, for his car. As he drove through West Hollywood to a canyon, they followed him to his address at the end of a long road sparsely populated with Spanish style houses. The Reverend's two-story abode was unique for the area, looking like a plantation mansion with grand Roman pillars in the front.

Fredrico was impressed. "He makes some good dough. Good." They both got out.

Only Carol walked down his driveway, passing cast iron statues of black men holding out real lanterns. She knocked. He answered. She said. "Can you please help me? My husband isn't here to help me and I can't lift my trunk door to my car. It's just too heavy for a lady, if you know what I mean. My husband can lift it real easy but I just am having trouble. Unless you have a bad back and I should find a knight in shining armor somewhere else."

"Oh no. But what were you doing out in these parts. They're restricted. So I who lives here."

Carol struck an aristocratic pose. "Oh? Well I was just going to paint pictures of the desert beauty of the canyon. Just down there a ways where I might find a flower or two on the cacti God created. And my easel and all my oils are in the back. I just love to paint pictures of God's creation as I pray to Him about how nice he made the world for us – you know – us white people who don't litter everywhere we go."

He smiled very big. His teeth were little. "I understand. Do you subscribe to our newspaper?"

"I love to read, of course, having gotten a proper education at Baptist Bible in Wichita Kansas. But - is your little paper about something important? I'm afraid this country is all being given away to the wetbacks and spooks and bone worshipers and it makes me so very very sad. After all the work we put into building this country, after all we white people have done. All they do is litter. They say the Jews are all really communist bankers. And the Eye-talians eat those most frightening heathen meatballs. So round. So round! I think they look indecent."

"Yes, meatloaf seems far more sensible, doesn't it, so I'm sure that's how God would like it. Since God likes us to be sensible. A moment please as I get for you a subscription card for our newspaper. I think you'll be very interested in it."

"You are so kind." She smiled, but in a way to be careful to hide her teeth, since that would show her true appearance, more. "My car is just across the street. Please don't be afraid. My easel doesn't bite. And I promise I won't paint anywhere near where I will disturb you. Sometimes I sing good ole Protestant hymns while I paint, and I don't sing as lovely as Jeanette MacDonald, I fear."

He huffed up his chest like he wasn't afraid of anything, and to Fredrico's car they marched. He asked, "You paint God's world often?"

Carol said, "You know - they have yet to find the proper paint color to represent a Chinese man's face. So those heathens have yet to be represented truly in the classical arts."

"Maybe you should write a column for my newspaper. You are

very factual when you speak."

Continuing to prattle idiotically, she added, "When I say flesh color we all know what I mean. The color of Jesus' face! Halleluiah!" Passing the car to get to the backseat, she commented, "See? Nobody inside. I'm all by my lonesome."

He put his chin out. "Don't fear."

"Now when I unlock this trunk, I want you to lift it very firmly and grip it as tight as you can because if it bounces back down, uncontrolled, it may jam badly like it did once before." She twisted the big silver key in the lock.

He grandly lifted the trunk. Fredrico was inside pointing a gun. He hopped out, ordering, "Inside."

"What's this?"

"Aye! We switch places, palsy." Fredrico pushed the reverend inside.

"I don't understand! You! You the Irish copper! You're drunk!"

Fredrico kicked Reverend Blanche back down as Carol angrily yelled, "Hail Mary, full of grace!"

Fredrico slammed the lid and they sped away. Fredrico asked her, "What took you so long? Didn't he believe you?"

"I wasn't gone long."

"You were too."

Carol said, "It seemed to be just a second, to me."

"I was waiting in the damn trunk forever while you just ran off at the mouth."

"I had to. It was a great scene! So much so that I just had to keep going on and on about what a Nazi person I am. I really got into the character of Madam Hitler. It was like I was in a war movie and I'm about to become a double agent. It was frightening so it was exciting, just like it would have been in real life. I didn't want it to end. I really felt something intense for the first time in a long time. Acting gives you feelings. I'm so good at this! I really would be a very good actress in a starring role where there is a lot going on."

"You're insane." Then he changed out of his copper uniform where he sat. Carol looked out the window in the other direction, wishing she'd hid her money somewhere completely out of the way so they could first spoon for awhile before they went on.

* * * * *

While driving through West Hollywood, a copper stopped them. "You forgot to use your turn signal back there."

The Reverend Blanche began to pound on his trunk lib. Carol began to stomp her foot to drown him out.

"What's with you, lady?"

"Cramps in my leg! Ooooh, cramps. Terrible cramps. My husband was taking me to the drugstore to buy some Epsom salts and we better go there in a hurry because I'm suffering here. Epsom salts and hurry! Ooooh. It's the only thing that works. Epsom salts and soda crackers!"

The cop asked, "What's soda crackers have to do with a cramp in your leg?"

"Nothing. I just like them!"

He backed away. "Go on, now, and drive careful."

Antonio made sure he backed up a ways so the noisy trunk wouldn't pass close by the cop. "So we're married now? I'm your husband? I'm your goddam husband but you won't even let me play with your knobbers?"

"Don't be a crumb. I had to do something. And fast. And don't touch me with them meat hooks of yours."

"I won't. Relax. You were brilliant."

"How long do you think it'll take to get any dough out of this guy, from his friends. And how much do you think they'll pay for him?"

"We'll have to be patient."

"And what do we do for dough in the meantime?"

"We?"

Carol said, "Of course. We're a team, now. Not married where you can paw me. A team where we just use our noggins."

"Well, we'll have to go hungry for a little while. I wish Antonio were here. He'd keep us all fat. He was the smart one who had the big plans."

Carol fumed. She didn't want to let him know she had a lot of money in her bra from the sale of Antonio's car. She didn't want to share. She opened her purse to show him it was empty of money. She pouted. "Since so far we're all copasetic, with the cops not breathing down our necks or anything right now, but we're so broke, let's just rob one bank. Just one. Just to tide us over for the next week."

Fredrico passionately shook his head. "No way. Bullets everywhere."

Carol stuck out her lower lip. "Awe. Come on."

"That's dollars to donuts. Long odds. Too long of an odds."

"Not if we do just one. They won't know what hit them. I'll go in with your bean shooter and you wait and be the driver."

Fredrico insisted, "No way. I'd never let you be in such danger."

"Awe, come on! I'm up to mustard for this, I'm sure. Nobody's going to do me in. I'm not in any real danger when they're confused because they weren't expecting a dame just to walk in like that and rob them. I have the element of surprise."

"What kind of bozo would let a doll like you go in there alone? That wouldn't be gentleman-like behavior from me at all."

Carol pointed out, "You have to drive anyway. We need a fast getaway and I sometimes get confused about what side of the street to be on. On a tractor in a big hay field all to yourself, you don't have that problem. So just because I can drive doesn't mean I'm very good outside a big hay field."

"Just one. We won't press our luck."

"And put your copper uniform back on. It might come in handy to confuse them if there's any witnesses. They'll think a cop went dirty and the FBI will begin by looking at the station for who done it."

"You got this all figured out."

She smiled big and touched her moles to make sure they were still stuck fast to her face. "Like a movie. Like a movie starring me.

And it'll have a happy ending because I said so. Then if you'd like we'll drive to Reno and get married for real. Then I'll have lots of babies and we'll never tell them what Mama did." She began to laugh.

"You're insane. I thought you were going to be a star."

"That too. Nowadays a star also has to be a mother to show she's normal. I'll be normal. Being normal is more scripted than any movie part. It's easy if you just try a little. Now there's a bank down there we passed before."

It was Wurdenbocker and Romrig Federal Savings and Trust, the same bank she had cashed in Michaels' car, so she thought she knew it well enough. "Just wait for me and I'll do a very normal bank robbery. I'll run out and we'll drive away. And everybody'll be so confused we'll get away with it."

"I have a bad feeling about this."

"You'll feel your part once we do it. Now right there. It's a little bank but it's a still a bank. Park right there. I'll run out that door and I can run fast enough so have the car already moving and I'll pop in from the running board. Got it?"

She ran in and out and he took off and she hopped in.

"You get any money? I hope so."

She opened her bag. "I see some in here."

He turned a corner and there was a cop car. They turned on their siren. "No!" He hit the gas and turned another corner, then another. The copper kept on his tail and began shooting. As Fredrico pushed Carol to the floor, their windows shot out. "No!" He turned another corner, went through a yard, went down an alley lined with garages, and turned alongside one. He hit the brake. The siren faded away. "We lost them." He jumped out and went to the other side and pulled Carol out.

She made a horrible expression. "We made it anyway."

"And we better have enough money for me to buy a new car. This one's all shot up!"

Carol shook her head. "They just put blank receipt tickets in my bag. We ain't got a penny."

"What?" He grabbed her purse.

"Careful. There's some makeup in there."

Fredrico yelled, "I never want to see you again! You're a curse on the family! You're a curse on this whole planet! I could kill you!"

Carol yelped and jumped to get out of the way. The car started to roll backwards. All by itself it rolled between two garages and into a flower garden, and then into a vast yard. It kept going until it plopped tail down into a swimming pool. Bubbles rolled up out of the trunk.

Carol said, "You forgot to set the parking break!"

"If I ever see you again, I'll kill you with my own two hands. I'll wring your scrawny little neck."

"Aw. That's not fair. I've been just ticketti-boo! A real sport. You ain't gonna find a palsy better then me that'll run in and out of a bank so fast for you like that. Let's just try it again!" She held out her hand. "Look. As cool as a cucumber! You need me."

Fredrico had to fight an urge to throttle her throat. "Now I'm going to walk home and you're not going to follow me. You're going just to go somewhere else to drop dead!" She watched him hurry to the pool. He splashed in, cursing, climbed into the tilted interior and pulled out his shirt. He changed his shirts as he walked away, so he wouldn't look like a copper anymore. Considering his mood, she dared not follow him. She touched her bra. It crinkled with the sound of money. She grinned at the idea of being so rich, but she didn't feel happy. She picked off her moles and pulled off her headscarf.

She walked through a Japanese Garden that was in the process of being bulldozed away. As she stood on a tall arched bridge over a pond of large goldfish, she watched them swim back and forth.

"Do you know what it feels like to be alive?" she asked them.

A bubble came to the surface.

"Oh my God! Oh no!" A memory suddenly came to her as if it was from far away. But it wasn't. "There's a man in the trunk of the car! In the pool! He is very very drowned by now!"

She felt her burning cheeks as she ran off, running through

freshly scraped dirt. She saw a billboard advertising Gone With The
Wind. It read, OPENING DECEMBER 14, 1939, ATLANTA,
THE MOST EAGERLY AWAITED FILM OF THE YEAR. The
sight of it made her burst into tears. She felt like the world was
passing her by.

"It's not fair!"

* * * * *

In a hotel room, Carol saw herself in the mirror and decided,
"You look like a horny piñata." She took her bra off and put all the
money in her purse. Then she bathed and slept and bathed again.
She couldn't wash away the feeling of being a dirty sinner. There was
a knock on the door. "Hello." She opened it, expecting it to be the
F.B.I. She blurted, "I'm a sinner. Oh. Who are you?"

"Have you read your Bible lately?"

Carol smiled. "Oh! A Bible salesman! How wonderful! Maybe
I can read about how to not be such a dirty sinner all the time! And
you're so handsome! Come in! Come in. Sit on the bed."

He smiled big, as if he'd never had it so easy. He opened his
briefcase. "Would you like a deluxe version?"

"I want one with the story of Sodom and Gomorrah."

"They all have that story. All of them."

Carol took the Bible he handed her and gave him some money.
"Where do I find the story?"

He admitted, "I have no idea. I just sell them. It's a best seller,
the Bible is. Everybody aught to have one. Or several. They should
be put all over the place."

"But you never read it?"

"Naw. Not really."

Carol admitted, "I'm so lonely. I can't bear to be alone. Reading
the Bible will be good for my soul. Maybe we can read it together.
Don't leave just yet. I hate being here in this room all alone. I feel
like the walls are going to fall in on me. Read to me about something
nice. No, read to me about sinners. I want some good sinning. I

want to read about something that takes my mind off of being so alone in this horrible world. Read to me all the sinning stories. "

"I have to go sell more Bibles."

"This was a fast sell. I didn't take any of your time. You can tell your boss I took a lot of convincing. Tell him what a sinful woman I was and how I just wouldn't listen for hours and hours."

"But you did buy a Bible right away."

Carol grabbed him. His case fell and Bibles fell out onto the floor. She pulled up his shirt. She pushed him down onto the bed. She grabbed his ribs and heaved, making it easy for him to roll over on top of her. "I'm a dirty sinner and I want you to stay with me!" She grabbed the back of his belt so he couldn't change his mind. She pulled him as tight to her as she could. "Never leave me! Never ever ever. Promise."

After he finished, he quickly redressed and left, and he hadn't been very long. Carol sat naked on the bed and opened her Bible and flipped carefully through it. She paused when she saw the heading, The Destruction of Sodom.

"Ooooh! Now I can finally find out what happened, and if the place is anything like Hollywood! I can read about how God puts sinners on fire." She was afraid of what she would read. Then she was merely shocked to read how the mob, young and old to the last man, surrounded Lot's house and yelled that they all wanted to rape the two angels who were visiting and getting ready for bed, and Lot told them that he wouldn't be so rude to his guests, even though they were angels and could just fly away, so he'd give the mob his two virginal daughters to rape all they wanted, instead. And then a bit later in the story Lot's family ran away as God set the cities up in flames even though all the men, small and great, had already been struck blind at Lot's door. Lot's wife turned into a pillar of salt just for looking back even though they'd been well warned that they'd be consumed by fire if they did anything at all like that. And then the father and his two daughters went to live in a cave because even though they were seasoned Sodomites they were afraid of yet another third city in the area called Zoar for reasons not given but they were just afraid – and - though they left with just the clothes on their back, there was plenty of wine in the cave. So the first daughter made her father get drunk with wine so she could make whoopee with him because she suddenly decided that there wasn't another man in all the earth and he was her only source of seed, even though Abraham and his very large camp full of men were very close nearby, not to mention Zoar, and the very next night the second daughter made her father drink wine so she could make him make whoopee with her for the very same reason.

Carol stopped reading. She was confused. It seemed that some very wicked people in the story escaped any punishment at all. And she wondered how a daughter could force her father to drink so much wine that he could lie with her. She'd had too much experience with drunken men to believe that for a heartbeat. It was as if the Bible story was making fun of anybody who would bother to read it, it was so crazy, and Carol was forced to wonder if there was some serious story behind this silly story that was the real story, but it had gotten hidden or lost, or was locked away in a church somewhere.

"This just can't be the Bible. It's too stupid! And the story should be called Sodom and Gomorrah and Zoar. And what were they doing in Gomorrah and Zoar that was so bad? And why was Zoar spared if it was too horrible to even be entered at all by somebody who was accustomed to Sodom?"

Suddenly Carol didn't feel like such a dirty sinner anymore - not with what was going on in the Bible. She decided she wouldn't feel bad anymore for what her brothers had done to her, if daughters and fathers did it in the Bible.

"Maybe my life would read even more crazy if put down on paper. I shouldn't be so harsh to judge – especially not the Bible. Who's to say how anybody's life would be if you had to read it."

She decided to take another bath and then to hop the streetcar to The Gold Rush.

* * * * *

"Mama Gravy! He's dead! Antonio was shot by a copper. I'm all alone in the world. What will I do? Can I bunk with Etienne?"

Mama Gravy looked down sadly. "She's gone."

"Oh? She get married, too?"

"No. She moonlighted with Ireland the Magician. And - "

Carl asked, "He made her disappear?"

"No! He cut her in half! The bastard!"

Carol was horrified. "Oh my! He can't do that and get away with it! Is he in jail? I hope?"

"In the hospital. He was so upset he shot himself in the head. He ain't a good shot."

Carol slapped her hands over her face. "Poor Etienne. I feel so odd. I was so jealous of her. I wanted to be a magic act star. I guess it ain't safe, huh?"

Mama Gravy said, "I already found new folks to share her old bunk."

Carol put her nose in the air. "Well I suppose it don't matter. I suppose I'm a little too old to be a dancehall hostess by now."

Mama Gravy laughed. "A whole year hasn't even passed since I first met you. You're still young and sweet. So young and sweet. A real doll. And look at you!" She grabbed her waist. "You've gained some weight. You look gorgeous. What have you been doing?"

"Eating three meals a day. It's great."

Mama Gravy slapped her behind. "And you look gorgeous. What do you say you share my warm bed?"

"You know I'm not homosexual."

"You can be whatever you want to be. It's your own movie that you star in. You've been such a rotten sinner, lately. It's time you sinned some more." She laughed very loudly.

Carol liked the sound of that. "Star in." She sat on the bed and was glad she'd long taken the money out of her bra since Mama Gravy was usually a very grabby person.

Mama Gravy left the room to change out of her dress. She swaggered back in, flapping her komodo open and shut. She went to the samovar and lit the coals underneath it. "Time for a cup of sassafras tea. It'll cure you of anything."

"Sure."

Mama Gravy put her ceramic pot on top of the metal urn, and then gasped, "Oh look at the clock! My favorite show has already started. A Guiding Light."

"I used to listen to that. It's been on two years now. I wonder where everybody is by now?"

Mama Gravy turned on her radio. "Shhh. Let me just hold you in my arms while I find out if that lowdown two-bit tramp is going to talk her way out of her own quicksand again, this time. She wants to marry one guy but likes another. The slut. It's all so Jane Austin, the dirty tramp."

After the show was over and the radio was back off, Mama Gravy asked, Carol, "Do you love me?"

"I – I don't' know."

"After all I did to you during the entire show - like no man has ever bothered to do – and you aren't sure you don't love me? Why look! Your knees are still knocking. Your bosom is pointing north and south."

"I know. And I feel my hair growing at record speed." She patted the top of her head.

"Then what's wrong? Why can't you say you don't love me?"

Carol searched her feelings. "It's just that it's hard for a person to know how they feel if what they're doing couldn't be a movie."

Mama Gravy crossed her eyes to show her exasperation. "Be a movie! That makes no sense."

Carol stated, "They don't make movies about two ladies in love."

"They also don't make movies where they show a guy and a gal jumping all over each other in bed."

"No. But you know it's there. You know they filmed it and other stuff, like taking a bath and brushing their teeth and going to the outhouse, like anybody, but they have to cut that all out before it can be shown in the theaters."

Mama Gravy was aghast. "You serious? You really think that?"

"Sure. And when I'm doing something that I know could be a movie - then I can feel it. If I'm doing something that I know can't be in a movie then I just don't know what to think – and I certainly don't know what to feel."

"You're insane."

"No I'm not. They don't make love story movies about two gals. I just know it."

Mama Gravy said, "And what about that movie you did that was never released at Republic? Did they ever film you going to the outhouse behind the ranch – as I'm sure that's all Republic has, a goddam hole in the ground, since they cater to Roy Rogers and Dale Evans. Was there a big window in the side of the outhouse for the camera to catch your every moment of real life?"

"No." Carol became very confused. "They only filmed the scenes they knew they would end up with when it would be projected in the theater. But they were being cheap."

"Everybody is cheap. At least they don't film the stars acting like real people going to the bathroom. Or brushing their teeth, for crying out loud. It's not real at all."

Carol insisted, "But they are real people. When they're playing those parts it's like it's more real than anybody. Real people on the streets are just nothing nobody shadows of people compared to Clark Gable and Franchot Tone. Now, they seem so real! Especially in a movie story. I bet even they don't look as good out on the street. You have to be on a big screen to really be real."

Mama Gravy said, "Well, at least if you're going to be insane like that, in that way, you're in the right town. In fact I bet that makes you in a majority and so that makes you normal. You're probably as loony as Betty Boop and she's the tops."

"Yeah, she's the best of them all. I bet she don't look like nothing unless she's up on the big screen, too, I bet."

Mama Gravy suddenly decided, "We need some reality. I don't know where to go find any, but we can go into the hills and see if that camp is still up there – that camp of all the dance hall hostesses I used to work with back in the twenties."

Carol looked at her, doubting. "Are you sure there's still anybody up there after all this time?"

"Probably not. But it'll be interesting to see. There'll probably be nobody up there so it'll just be a nature hike – plus some goddam weeds."

Carol darkened. "I've never been on a nature hike before. It sounds awful. I used to walk around the ugly sheep farm that I grew up on enough to not need to do that now, I don't think."

Mama Gravy playfully slapped her arm. "This will not be a sheep farm that's ready to fall off the edge of the earth into Canada. This is a hike into the Hollywood Hills."

Chapter Ten

Dressed as men so they'd be comfortable, they took the streetcar up Mulholland Drive and then transferred to the Mount Olympus streetcar and went into Laurel Canyon, heading north. Mama Gravy kept pointing out to where the houses were only on one side of the street, "I wonder if that was Houdini's house? It could be that one. I bet it's that one. Oh, look at that house. That one is grand. I bet that was Houdini's house. I bet it was. I can just feel it. I can feel his spirit. His spirit is still here."

Carol gave her a doubting expression. "His spirit? I thought he was the one who debunked spiritualists as frauds and fakes. He wrote a book about it. Miracle Mongers and their Methods I never got a chance to read it but people sure talked about it a lot, and it was in all the magazines."

Mama Gravy pursed her lips tightly together, and then finally said, "Oh. That's right."

They got off before the streetcar continued on out the other side of the canyon to the San Fernando Valley, where it looked desolate. A dusty rabbit ran off in a mad dash to get away from them. Carol asked, "Is the Mojave Desert just over that ridge?"

"Oh god, I hope not. Now where are we? Everything looks so different." After a few steps, Mama Gravy pretended to want to faint. "Oh, I forgot how spread out everything is. Back in the good old days there was a trolley that ran all the way from Sunset Boulevard to the top of Lookout Mountain Road. Up over there. You can't see it from here but it's up there."

"The trolley?"

"No. The road. The trolley stopped in 1918. How stupid. Just when the real tourists come, they stop it. We have to walk it now. Let's find some walking sticks. It's always good to have something to poke ahead of you to scare away the snakes."

Carol looked around. "I don't see any tracks for a trolley."

"It was one of those trolleys that didn't run on tracks." Picking up two nice long branches along the way, they had walking sticks. Mama Gravy said, "I hope the roads are all where they're supposed to be. I hope I don't get lost and we die and are left like some dustbowl cow bones."

"We won't die. You have enough supplies in your bag to feed an army. And I know what cacti are edible." Carol smiled proudly.

"If somebody's still up there in that camp, I want to bring presents. Don't you think they'd love a tin of crackers? It sure beats lizard guts every day."

Carol asked, "Why would there be a road if it's just a camp?"

"I only need the road to get us up and out that way. I hope the road is still there, and then the trail. And then you just walk through weeds and rocks for awhile." Mama Gravy moaned. "I hope I'm not too old to make it."

Carol chuckled at her. "Don't be silly. I love the air out here. It smells like flowers. Dry hot flowers."

"God I need a cigarette. I can't breathe."

Carol said, "Then have one."

"I was going to save the box of them for the presents. I may change my mind. By the time I get there they may just get an empty box."

Carol laughed.

Mama Gravy admitted, "I'm nervous about meeting people who've been living out in the wild for ten years."

"You and me both. What if they don't even speak our same language anymore."

"After how I last saw them, praying to weeds and bushes, and painting themselves with mud, they may not. We may just have to point and laugh."

They walked a while longer without conversing so Mama Gravy could put her concentration into huffing and puffing as they went up a great slope. All she said was, "Watch for snakes and falling rocks," a few times. A large iguana on a boulder bobbed his head angrily at them before slipping away. Then they walked along a meandering path to get through a field of stubborn vegetation twisted with wind and drought. Mama Gravy sadly said, "We're here."

It was plain to see where the camp was and it was plain nobody had been there in a long while. Two of the huts had fallen over. Three were upright but only one had its woven twig roof still on. There was a large drying rack or a skinning rack construction that was leaning. Yellow grassy weeds grew everywhere, undisturbed.

Carol was relieved. "Nobody's home."

Mama Gravy desolately muttered, "The evocative nature of ruins."

"What was that?"

"Just a saying. Look at it. How sad it all looks." She walked up to where there had once been a fire circle. Stones were nicely chosen and piled to fashion a wide low fence encircling it. "No fire has burned here for awhile." She picked up a handmade clay bowl that had been baked black. "No ants or nothing. Gone for a while."

"Carol said, "I wonder how long?"

"Well that answers it. Nobody is left. I wonder where they went? You just can't live out here like this for this long and then go back into town one day and work anywhere. Unless the studios decide to make a lot of movies about cave women, I don't know. Look for any graves." They walked around the site for a while. Mama Gravy finally said, "Not even anything that looks like a grave."

Carol asked, "Should we just head back to town, then?"

"Let's stay the night."

"What? I'd be scared!"

Mama Gravy asked, "Haven't you ever camped out before?"

"No."

"Well, it's about time."

"I don't see the point."

Mama Gravy said, "It's an American thing to do. Every year everybody goes somewhere else other then where they are, only because they're sick of their own bed. After a bad night's sleep on the ground you love a real bed again. It works like a charm."

"Are you sure?"

Mama Gravy nodded. "This country is great because everybody is filled with appreciation and where does that appreciation come from? From sleeping on the hard cold ground once a year. From camping."

Carol felt nervous. "But, I've never not loved a real bed. I've always been very grateful. I've always worried that someday I might not have a bed – or anything else. I don't need to go camping to learn to like anything with all my heart."

"I need a break from the Gold Rush. We're camping out for the night and that's that. We have lots of provisions and I don't even have to share my marijuana with anybody."

* * * * *

It grew dark. There was an eerie silence over the land until the sun was completely gone and the sky was a dark purple splattered with winking stars. Then percussive yipping exploded from the east. Mama Gravy hugged herself. "Oh, no! Coyotes!"

Carol assured her. "They won't bother us if we stay at the fire. I'm glad I don't have to worry about any sheep herds right now."

"You had vermin troubles with your sheep?"

"Of course. Wolves and coyotes always wanted a sheep snack. We wouldn't let them, of course, but it took some work. Especially in the winter when everything got desperate."

"I wonder if they'll get close enough to see."

"Maybe." Carol explained, "But then they goofed. They don't like to be seen. So if you really want to upset them, let them know you're looking right at them when they get too close."

Mama Gravy rubbed her arms. "You're giving me the frights!"

"It was your idea to go camping. Where are you going to go camping where there ain't no vermin? Vermin don't scare anybody. It's just vermin."

"Let's talk about something else."

Carol gasped. "I saw eyes over there! The fire caught the whites of their eyes! Eyes of at least six people."

Mama Gravy yelled, "Hey! Who's there! If you got some moonshine, you better share it with me or I'll go punch your lip!"

"No. They're gone."

"How do you know? Maybe they just stepped back out of sight."

"No. They lights of their eyes just went straight up."

"Up into the sky?"

Carol looked up into the stars. "Yeah, I guess so."

"I better stop blowing my reefer smoke in your face."

"No. I really did see it."

"It was just the reefer making you dizzy. That's all. And making you stupid. That's what reefer does best."

Carol asked, "Then why smoke it? Why make yourself stupid?"

Mama Gravy looked thoughtfully at her smoldering cigarette. "I often get tired of hearing myself think. I just want to stop the voices in my fool head. Reefer helps. It puts a thick pillow between me and the voices and muffles them out a bit. Reefer is God's way of helping us slow down when we're too worked up to do it all for ourselves. Reefer is God's way of letting us know he cares about us."

They heard a stick break. Carol said, "Did you hear that?" A light flashed in the sky. "Did you see that?"

"Just a little heat lightening, I bet. Don't worry. Enjoy nature when it's a light show in the sky. I think I need to blow a lot more of this smoke in your face."

A strong wind picked up. Carol and Mama Gravy moved into the hut that was in the best condition. Carol said, "I hope the roof doesn't blow off."

"It hasn't yet and I bet there's been worse windstorms."

"What's that sound?"

"Is that the wind?"

Carol said, "I hear singing. Or chanting. A bunch of women!"

They ran out and looked around and didn't see anybody, but they still heard the women and the sound was coming from straight above them in the sky.

Carol asked, "What are they singing? Is there a hot air balloon up there?"

"In this wind? It wouldn't hover. There's no hot air balloon. It's just singing up there above the wind."

"That's impossible!"

Mama Gravy asked, "What are they singing?"

"Are they?"

"I can't make out the words. Is it raining? I feel something on my cheek. It's wet."

"I don't feel any rain. The air is so dry. Oh god, I'm scared. Let's go back home now."

Mama Gravy pointed out, "We'd fall going down the canyon. We have to wait until the sun comes back out."

"I can't wait that long! I'm terrified! I just peed on my leg!"

"You'll break your leg if you go anywhere right now."

They hurried back to the hut and hoped they wouldn't be murdered.

When the sun rose, they stepped back outside. In the yellow glow, it was like nothing had happened. A small brown songbird flew from bush to bush, happily chirping. But then Carol noticed Mama Gravy's face and she jumped.

Mama Gravy asked, "What?"

"Your cheek!"

Mama Gravy rubbed it. "What is it?"

"Mud!" Carol decided not to mention that it looked painted on with a finger, in a careful spiral. "It's just mud." She knew Mama Gravy would blame her.

"Oh. Is that all?"

"Yeah, just some mud. That's all."

Mama Gravy asked, "Then why did you look like you'd been a monster?"

"I'm just jumpy."

"I'd say. Oh, camping out is so dirty. Let's eat everything I brought and then get the hell out of here."

Carol said, "And we didn't hear any women singing last night."

"Of course not. We were just full of too much reefer. And

imagination. And we're damn fools. Not another word."

"My lips are buttoned tight."

"I'll never smoke dope again."

* * * * *

When they got back to the Gold Rush, they went into the bedroom. Mama Gravy locked the door as she said, "There. Now I feel safe. No more adventures for me. No more vacations. No more! I need a cup of tea. And bad." She lit the coals under her samovar. "Sassafras, of course. It'll purge the devil right out of us, and I'm sure we had the devil all around us. We'll sweat and pee until all the devil poison in us is gone."

Carol scoffed. "But you weren't in any danger, ever, were you? Maybe you were in danger of falling off a cliff at some point, but that was all."

"We heard the devil! You know it."

Carol nodded. "Heard something."

"Devils even, maybe! I feel it all in me now, like I need a bath. A good cup of tea will clean the devil out, I'm sure."

Carol insisted. "We did not see the devil. And we didn't hear a thing. Remember we didn't? We agreed we didn't?"

Mama Gravy put her ceramic pot on top of the metal urn. "My memory is still playing it back to me like a bad radio owned by Bela Lugosi." She blew on the coals to hurry them up.

"We decided we didn't hear a thing. So we didn't."

"You say that so easily. You look so peaceful. I'm a wreck!"

Carol shrugged. "When terrible things happen, you just say they didn't and then who can say they did? And you move on."

"Oh?"

Carol said, "What else can you do?"

"It's not that simple."

"It is if you say it is. The whole world is only in your own head, anyway, so just make it want you want."

Mama Gravy stomped her foot. "What made you not only such

a hardboiled egg but a rotten egg, too? Here, smoke some dope with me and it'll get you talking."

"I don't smoke dope."

"You do now. It'll open you up so that you finally make some sense and say what you mean. Here. I'm not going to blow it in your face this time. You're going to smoke dope properly like a normal person, like everybody else. Do like I do."

Carol did. "Yuck. That tastes like - I feel dizzy. I feel – light. I feel something odd. My eyes feel dry. How do you scratch your peepers?"

"Put your hands down. You'll blind yourself. Here. You just need more dope. It'll get the devil out of us."

"Oh. Thanks. It tastes better, now. Wait a minute. Take it all back. I can't feel my legs. I can't feel my arms! I feel? Happiness? I think I feel happy, but I'm not sure. It's like the worries just somehow all went away. Away. Hold me. I'm happy. I like that feeling. It's the best feeling anybody can ever have. I like feeling happy. It's like when I was eight years old and I got a piece of candy at Christmas and I was so happy about it before it even went in my mouth."

Mama Gravy said, "You feel happy? You're doped up, that's for sure. So tell me, happy lady, why are you such a sinner?"

Carol giggled. "I am not. I got married."

"As if that patched anything up in your life. A wayward girl usually starts off as wayward as a kid. And it's usually her father that has abused her and that's why she ends up feeling so bad about her self that she just throws her whole life away on the streets. A girl with a good daddy rarely does that."

"My daddy never abused me. Well, he did make me eat rat poison a few times. But that was to kill the baby."

Mama Gravy gasped.

"I never told anybody before because it was so terrible, but now that I feel like I'm floating and I don't care anymore, yeah, he did it. He made me eat rat poison to kill my two babies."

"Your Daddy was the Daddy?"

"No, even though Daddy always locked my bedroom door and

window so that I was locked away inside, my brothers were always climbing in through the shudders somehow. Six of them, so who knows who of them was the daddy, but they would all say the same thing as if they planned it. Let's practice being married. You gotta practice everything in life. And they would take out their animal parts on me. They were animals in lots of ways."

"And your Daddy let that happen?"

"Well, he did lock me up to try. The room was so small that the door didn't even open all the way before it hit the bed. And there was no light. I was locked away all one winter. They put extra straw in there to help keep me warm. I lived curled up in a little dark straw cave. My brothers would come in and gag and cough and say I smelled so bad but then they'd always leave me smelling worse. So I'd just lay there and I'd think about what it felt like to be alive. I didn't really feel all the way alive. But I didn't know what to think about it. I didn't know what to think about anything. It's hard to think when you're like that. I still don't know how to think about it, though I think about it all the time."

"Where was your Daddy during all this?"

"He was somewhere. And he did whip my brothers all the time. They were always in trouble about everything and always getting whipped. And Daddy would say that he'd wished he'd kept us all in church after Mamma died, so we'd have the fear of God in us. But my brothers said that Hell was just a place made up by parents to try and scare naughty kids like them into behaving. And they didn't want to behave. They just wanted to have fun."

"Rat poison can kill you."

"No. Daddy said it only kills things the size of rats. And we had to hope the baby in me wasn't any bigger than a rat or else we'd have a born baby, and incest in the family, and that would be a great shame, and the neighbors would shun us. I couldn't have that. My neighbor over the hill was a real gentleman. He paid me real money to drive his tractor while he pitched the hay in the wagon I was pulling. I didn't want him to know anything bad had happened to me, no matter what. I liked driving his tractor for money. It was really hard to steer that thing, but – what was I talking about?"

"Rat poison."

"Oh. Daddy."

Mama Gravy guessed, "The rat poison made you so sick you thought you'd die, I bet. I bet you almost died if it was enough to kill the baby inside you. It takes a lot of anything to kill a baby. The body has a lot of ways of protecting the baby from things. Even poison."

"Oh yes, I was so sick one hot summer that I wouldn't be able to get out of bed for a week, or even sit up. Or even shoo away the flies. And Daddy wasn't good at being a nursemaid so I'd lie there so thirsty I think it did drive me insane. And my bed smelled like the outhouse. It was so terrible. Lucky we had straw beds so we could always dump it and start over with fresh straw. But it was terrible for that week. And then the dead baby would come out and it would be so horrible. And daddy wouldn't call the doctor. He said it was a shame what I'd done and if the baby would kill me with it, it was only justice. And then I would have a few weeks of not being able to walk. I would just crawl around to get anywhere and Daddy would say that I was on my knees in front of Jesus."

"Your Daddy was a rat. A big rat. No wonder you're so off the rails. And your brothers are the worse bozos I've ever heard of. They should just be all hit very hard in the head with a very big hammer."

Tears dropped out of Carol's eyes. "I never told anybody this before. It doesn't sound real to my own ears for some reason. Like it really is too terrible to have happened. I was so little when this all started. And then a year later, when I had my first menstruation, that's when the first baby started and daddy locked me away and put me to bed with my first box of rat poison. That first time was spring. We had just finished picking peas. Most of the time we spent in the pea garden I wasn't picking peas. Neither were my brothers."

Mama Gravy said, "That's the most horrible thing I've ever heard, and I've heard a lot of sorry girls spill their guts all over me."

"I wonder if that's why Daddy made sure that tractor rolled over his head. Maybe he knew that if he was dead then everything would be sold and we'd all have to go our own ways. Maybe Daddy died to save me. Maybe my Daddy was like Jesus and he gave his life to save mine. I never thought of it that way before." Carol started to bawl. "My Daddy! My Daddy! He died to save me!"

"He was a rat."

"He was Jesus!"

"You suffered."

"Everybody suffers. But then I was saved."

"Not like that."

Carol calmed down. "Well, I moved far away from them all, to be so far away from them it would be like they didn't exist. I don't care to know how they're doing. Not at all. I just know that if I become a star and get rich and my brothers think they can all come and live with me, I'll slam my big fat door in their faces. I won't even let them get past the gate. I'll have my butler go throw ice water on them all, through the bars."

"That's all you can do. Stay away."

"Life only goes in one direction. Soon it'll be the forties and who knows where I'll be. A girl don't need any family if they're so bad. Anything that's bad has to be ran away from. Except this good dope. This is good. I didn't realize how good dope is. I really do feel happy. I can't believe it. It's so wonderful to feel happy. I want to be doped up every minute of my life if this is how it's going to make me feel! Whoopeeeee!"

"You're finally growing up."

"Sure," Carol agreed. "But I don't ever think I'll ever shake the most horrible thing I remember from that farm, no matter how old I live"

"Your rotten brothers weren't rotten enough? What could top that?"

Carol nodded fervidly. "Yes, they were rotten - rotten, rotten - taking their turns humping me like I was nothing but something to hump. But they didn't try and eat me."

"What? Who tried to eat you, sugar-pie?"

"Nobody tried to eat me. It was the family dog."

Mama Gravy gasped. "A dog tried to eat you?"

"No! It ate the rabbit."

"Oh. You're just joshing now, and getting even more boring than that, now. That happens every day. And I thought you had a news flash."

Carol said, "No. The rabbit was still alive. It was right in the front yard. And the dog was eating its back legs for some reason. Usually a dog shakes a rabbit to death before it eats it. But this rabbit was just stunned and when it tried to hop off, it was real sluggish, so the dog just pulled it back to the same place and nibbled some more. And then after a few minutes the rabbit would try it again and try to hop away and the dog would pull it back to the same spot to eat some more, again. I yelled at Dad to kill the rabbit and Dad said the dog was just having some fun, and even a dog should have some fun once or twice in his life."

"Your Dad had a way with words, did he?" Carol looked off. "I even still dream that horrible image of the rabbit being eaten alive like that. It was so horrible. The sight of it will never leave my eyes. I felt so sorry for that poor rabbit. And that dog was a mean buzzard."

Mama Gravy stated, "You came to the wrong town if you don't like things getting eaten alive. You're in Hollywood. Metaphorically it's more of a rule than an exception for the cannibals to be in full trot as they bite off of each other. And sharks. And the fans. Yes, the fans. It will become literal, soon, I bet. It's in the air."

Carol asked, "What are you talking about?"

"Soon the fans that show up for the premieres will just eat the stars."

"No."

"Sure. Now the fans are just ripping little bits of a star's clothes and hair out. But soon it'll just escalate and fans will start wanting bits of flesh, too."

Carol disagreed. "You exaggerate. That's malarkey. Fans just want autographs."

Mama Gravy gently patted the side of the teapot to see if it was getting hot. "That was last year's news. Now they're going for a little more. And next month it'll even be a little bit more. And when it goes too far, at one of those overcrowded premiers where they make everybody wait too long and they get mad, it won't be like your poor rabbit. It'll be all over in a flash. A mob will be running off with their own souvenir of flesh and bones and some poor miss movie star will only be a wet spot left behind on that red carpet, if they don't take the carpet, too."

Carol shivered, speechless. "Well. Golly."

Mama Gravy reiterated, "Those premieres are getting too out of hand. Too dangerous. Mark my words. I'm always right about these things"

* * * * *

While waiting in a long line to see The Women, Mama Gravy spoke to Carol in a tone loud enough for everyone around them to hear. "I bet this film flops. Just flops. Who wants to see Joan Crawford as a bitch? Nobody. Not even her most loyal fans who think they can handle anything."

Carol said, "We're here its second week and look how long the line is! You'd think this was the premiere it's so crowded. Still."

"It'll pass. Nobody wants to see a movie that's all women. Women want to see Cary Grant take Gary Cooper's clothes off. If I want to see a bunch of women being bitchy I'll go to the butcher shop where they try and save pennies on a scrap of shackles."

Carol slipped her fat beret back to wipe her forehead. "It's so hot out here. I thought the nights were supposed to get cool. Not tonight. Why does it have to always be such bad weather when I'm trying to go out and do something."

"Why are you always wearing that same hat these days? You wear nothing else. You practically sleep in it."

Carol resituated it nervously. "It's my style. My look. I like it."

"Nobody wears a hat at night. Don't you know fashion?"

Carol pushed down on it. It made a slight crunching sound. She said forcefully. "It's my look!"

* * * * *

While waiting in a long line to see The Wizard of Oz, Mama Gravy spoke to Carol in a tone loud enough for everyone around them to hear, "Who wants to see Judy Garland try to play a little girl. How perverted. Nobody wants to see that."

Carol responded, hugging herself against the violent night wind. "Well, the premiere was a few weeks ago and look how at how many people are here? Still. It's a really big hit!"

"Nobody wants to see old vaudeville hams play parts like this. People want to see Cary Grant playing with Gary Cooper's ding-a-ling!"

A woman put her hands over her daughter's ears. "I never!"

Mama Gravy agreed. "I never, either. And it's a shame."

Carol's beret blew off. She screamed bloody murder and dove for it. "Give it to me! Give it to me! Now! It's mine! Mine! Give it to me!"

Mama Gravy looked sideways at Carol as if she was ready for a straightjacket. "Nobody wants to steal your damn hat." She turned back to the offended woman. "And they say Dorothy sings in the barnyard and it was so ridiculous the producer tried to cut it but the director made a stink to keep it in, the sap. You know what they say: when in doubt, take it out. When poor Judy starts singing in the barnyard, you know we're all going to start howling. Poor Miss Garland's career is over." She turned back to Carol. Let go of your damn hat. If it blows off again, just go pick it up again."

"I won't let it."

* * * * *

While waiting in the cold rain in a long line to see Gone With the Wind, Mama Gravy spoke to Carol in a tone loud enough for everyone around them to hear, "Who wants to see a war movie in a time like this? Doesn't anybody know what's going on in Europe? And they say the whole second half of the picture is as slow as molasses in the wintertime. It's just those two actors talking to each other."

Carol just thought about how crowded it was, with the line so long and thick. This film was obviously a hit. She also worried about her beret getting wet so she pushed up even closer to Mama Gravy, who was holding the umbrella.

"Nobody wants to see war, and the newspaper even dismissed the whole thing as nonsense. I read in the Hollywood Reporter that you have the Civil War with just a few Negroes as sidekicks, and so they ignored what the whole Civil War was about. And Irving Thalberg said right to Louis B. Mayor's face, Forget it, Louis, no Civil War picture ever made a nickel."

A woman angrily turned to Mama Gravy and stated, "It don't matter about all that. It's a story about Scarlet and Rhett and it's a swell one at that. That's all that matters."

Chapter Eleven

The next day, Carol did the dishes with Mama Gravy. The radio talked about how the small corn of the Red Indians was through. It was now a big new scientific world of something called hybrids.

Mama Gravy said, "Ain't that just something, maybe they can start that hybrid technique on people. God knows they need improving. And they could use that hybrid technique on the movies. They need help. And if we could just hybrid dishes to not need washing." There was a knock on the door. "I got it." Mama Gravy walked outside and talked a short while.

When she returned to help with the drying, Carol asked, "Who was that?"

"Some door-to-door type. A real lady. But she was selling suntan lotion. What the heck would I do with that? I don't go out in the sun. Not on your life. But it did smell good. Good enough to eat. Like coconut cream pie. Oh God! Now I'm so hungry for coconut cream pie!"

Carol asked, "So you didn't buy any?"

"The lotion? No way. She said it had coffee in it. She said she ground it as fine as dust in a special electric machine. I told her I only drink the stuff."

Carol asked, "Was it Rita Sunshine's suntan lotion?"

"How'd you know?"

"Rita Sunshine herself drove me into this crazy town."

Mama Gravy said, "Oh, then it's good she's doing well."

"She said so? She told you that?"

Mama Gravy explained, "No. But you can tell those things. She didn't look hungry. She had a nice new clean dress. Her hat was so cute it could pee kittens. She didn't care at all to hard sell me. I told her how I hated the sun and she seemed to want to talk to me about how I might get rickets if I didn't get any at all. All my bones might shrink. She told me sun was good for people, like suddenly she was more interested in selling me a bit of what was up there in the sky. She told me her lotion was for people who get too much sun. She could have lied and made promises about her lotion that would make it like it would cure me of everything including snakebites and avalanches. You know how people are."

Carol was relieved. "I'm so glad she seemed to be doing okay. It was so kind of her to pick me up and drive me here. So I only want the best for her."

"Oh, better than okay. I can tell by these things. I'm never wrong."

"You are too wrong. Sometimes – about things."

"But never about another dollface. I can size up a woman in a heartbeat." The door knocked again. Mama Gravy yelled, "Come in!"

"I'll get the door in case it's Rita Sunshine again, and she's come back, and I want to say hi."

Fredrico let himself in. He looked in irritation to Carol and said, "So there you are."

"You could say hi a little nicer. You still sore at for when I made monkeys out of you and me?"

"You."

Carol laughed nervously. "You know what I mean."

Fredrico said, "I knew I could find you here."

"Where else could I be? Mama Gravy has been my only friend."

"There's going to be a New Year's Eve party at Mama Caltanisseta's."

Carol asked, "Can I invite my friend, Mama Gravy, along? She's my only friend."

"That wet sock."

Carol said, perkily, "Awe. Come on! She's kippy!"

"That two-bit whore."

"Hey! What is it anyway with saying something's bad for being two-bit? That's fifty cents! That's a lot! And a working girl only gets twenty-five cents a pop, anyway. A two-bit whore should be something pretty good, by my math."

Fredrico said, "No. It's just the Caltanisseta family at this party. Nobody else. Us brothers that are left, you the widow, and Mama."

"Oh. Sweet," Carol said facetiously, frowning. She went to the bedroom where Mama Gravy was glued to the radio.

"You're not invited."

"Shhh.

"I'm invited to a New Year's Eve party. But you're not invited."

Mama Gravy looked at her. "Then tell them to jump off a cliff."

"It's the brothers that are left. It's just a family thing. I'm the widow."

Mama Gravy said, "Oh. Them. Tell that Mama Cow Town Poinsettia to kiss my feet."

Carol corrected her, "Mama Caltanisseta."

"Whatever. I still think I said it better."

"I've never been invited to a party before."

"What?"

Carol shook her head sadly. "I have never been invited to a party before, not nothin'. Unless you count my own wedding party. I was invited to that by my husband, I guess. But it just seems if you're invited to a party, you should be grateful. Even if it is just a family thing. I don't know." She looked at her feet.

Mama Gravy waved her off. "Then go and be a dizzy blonde all on your own. Eat spaghetti and be happy. I don't need to run out to a party every New Year's Eve. I'll just relax this year. I'll listen to the party on the radio."

* * * * *

New Year's Eve, Carol tried to say good-bye to Mama Gravy, but couldn't find her anywhere around The Gold Rush. "Awe, she went out and found a real party to go to."

She got in Fredrico's new car, making sure she didn't comment on it because he was probably still sore from when his last one slipped backwards into a swimming pool with somebody in the trunk that they may have gotten some good money out of. They didn't talk to each other about anything the whole ride but listened to the radio. Bob Wills and the Texas Playboys were broadcasting live from a party. Carol watched the city lights go by and thought about how it all seemed dreamlike and unreal at such a dark hour.

Finally Fredrico parked and said, "We're here."

Carol stepped out of the car on the other side of a playground and saw a frightening thing. Though it was dark, a man was dancing among the swings with his hand on his hip while shaking his head like he was pretending it was full of big bouncy curls. He sang over and over again, in a mock child's voice, "Good ship lollypop. Good ship lollypop. Good ship lollypop!"

Walking up to the apartment building, Carol became even more frightened. "What party? Not much of a ring-a-ding-ding, huh. It seems so quiet up there."

Fredrico said, "It's just the family at Mama Caltanisseta's. Those of us who are still around. Remember? No friends."

"Sure."

"Wait." They stepped into the enclosed back porch that led to the back hall. The old paint had crocodiled. He took her arm to stop her.

"What?"

"Before we go upstairs and join the family, one of my brothers told me he wants to talk to us here."

"In the back hall?" She looked around and noticed some furniture left behind. "This isn't a fun place for anything."

Fredrico's brother whispered something in his ear. He looked at Carol in alarm, and then nodded, then acted resigning, and then he left.

Carol moved to follow Fredrico, but his brother said, "You stay right there, dollface."

"Why?"

Fredrico's brother pulled out a gun and aimed it at her. "Kiss your keester goodbye."

"What? Why!"

"You're not too much of a whiz-kid. Not at all. You screwed up real bad. You screwed the family over with bad advice that cost us MGM and millions. We've killed for less."

Carol said, "Well - now that MGM is so prosperous, take it now. Those movies ended up doing real good."

"The plan only had a narrow window of time. It's too late now. It's too late to do anything but be sorry. It's too late for us. It's too late for you."

Carol pleaded, "No! Still try your plan. Then if you run MGM, you can make me a star. Your brother would want that. But your plan probably wouldn't have worked, anyway. If it was so easy, somebody else would have already done it. You just can't muscle in one a movie studio. I don't care how good you blackmail a few producers. It's just too insane of a pipe dream."

"You say we're stupid or something?"

Carol got angry. "I say you all dream too big. All you Caltanisseta brothers. You'd never take over a movie studio. That was dollars to donuts if I ever heard the expression. You'd never bleed them out of anything. You'd just get shot full of daylight for the trying, and that's all folks. And I was hoping it would get me to be a star. But that's silly. There was never a chance you'd take over MGM and make me a star. Never. Planting a dead body in somebody's swimming pool? That gets you nothing but a dead body in a swimming pool!"

"Dollface, the only thing you're going to star in is your own funeral."

A gun went off but it wasn't his. He dropped his gun. He looked down in horror at the blood coursing out of his shirt. He dropped dead. Fredrico ran in and looked surprised to see that Carol was the one standing. Another shot went off and Fredrico's eyeball blew out as he dropped dead.

"What crumbs." Mama Gravy stepped out of the shadows of a stairway leading to the basement.

Carol was very surprised. "You!"

Two other brothers ran down, shouting, "What happened?"

Mama Gravy re-aimed. They were both plugged in the heart. The final brother noisily ran down the stairs with a Tommy gun already firing. The two women pounced back to the shadows of the basement door before he could spot them. When he ran out of ammo, and the porch wall was all ventilated left to right, Mama Gravy shot him in the head. It didn't kill him but he was mighty stunned. He came at them like he would rip them apart with his hands. They stepped aside, hugged the wall, and he tripped down the stairs. At the bottom he got up.

Mama Gravy said to him, "Here, you need some of the hair of the dog that bit you." She opened her gun and put a few more bullets in and shot him again until he finally fell.

Carol asked, "Why'd you have to kill them all?"

"You don't want a brother left alive with a vendetta against me."

"You?"

"For telling you about the movies doing bad, and then they didn't."

Carol admitted, "I didn't tell them you told me. I made it sound like I was the one who was so smart."

Mama Gravy looked at her gun in dismay. "So I killed them for nothing. My hide was fine."

Carol hugged her. "Oh. You saved me!"

"Yep. I saved your hide again. Aren't you one to find trouble. Come on. Let's get out of here before the coppers show up."

From the top of the steps they heard Mama Caltanisseta. "Hello? Anybody still alive down there?"

Mama Gravy yelled up to her, "No!"

"Oh crap."

They ran out and hopped a streetcar going up Santa Monica Boulevard. Carol continued, "That is so nice that you saved my life."

"Like I cared? Maybe I do. Maybe I just got used to you. And I was so upset that I made such a big mistake about how badly MGM would do. I couldn't believe I was so wrong. I've never been wrong about things before. It drove me so bananas that I was wrong that

I couldn't sleep, I was so mad. Then I thought about how you had told me that you took my advice and got all them Sicilian brothers to call off their plan to take MGM, because you got them to think that all their pictures coming out would all be wet socks. And I knew that you can't be wrong about that kind of thing and not have them want some revenge for it. Not with your husband dead and not with you having no real protection anymore. His brother is not the same thing. So I did it for you because I really did it for me. I just couldn't stand being so wrong."

"I still don't quite understand. But I think I do. When you're a hothead, it makes sense." Then Carol put her hand over her mouth like she just had a naughty thought.

"What."

"Mama Caltanisseta! Who's left to keep her up in that expensive apartment like a queen? Or will she have to go live out on the street."

"Her boys were all rotten crooks. A regular pack of Hollywood sinners. Serves her right." Mama Gravy chuckled cruelly.

"She was nasty to me but that doesn't mean I want anybody out on the street. I ate her food. The poor old woman. She doesn't even know English but I ate her delicious food. Well that's over. The end of an era."

"If she doesn't know our language then she can go back home. We speak English here and sometimes we're really loud. Hey!" Mama Gravy finally noticed the street they were going down. "We're on the wrong line. We want to go that way. The Gold Rush is that way."

Carol shook her head. "I'm not going back to that place. I'm going to join the nuns at the Franciscan convent. I've had enough of this life. There's just something terrible and out of balance about it all. I can't keep living like this."

Mama Gravy nodded. "I hear you. I wanted to be a nun, once. Yep, even a nun. I was all over the place when I was young, wanting this and wanting that, and trying to do it all to see what it was. From day to day I'd be a different person, trying everything new, trying to find something that fit. My life was just a story that made no sense, it was so all over the place – but I guess that's how it is with all young people. I wasn't so special."

"Why didn't you become a nun?"

"I talked myself out of it. Nuns don't do all the dope I do. I just couldn't live without all my dope. But you seem to mainly get high on a big tall bowl of spaghetti and a bottle of wine. You'd fit right in."

Carol said, "You can do without the dope. I know you can. Come on and join me and be a nun with me. It'll be fun, and it'll be a lot better than what we let all the bozos do to us in the backroom of The Gold Rush."

"Maybe next year I'll be ready to be a nun."

Carol warned her, "Maybe by then you'll be dead."

"Then the Reaper finds me with my pants down. What can I do? But I just can't do it now. If you want to, that's your business. And pray for me all you want, but not to give up the dope. I just love it too much. In fact, the more I think about it, the more I want some right now. I'll see you later. Maybe I'll see you later in Hell."

"Nuns go to Heaven."

"Everybody says they want to go to Heaven for the climate, but they all end up in Hell for the company."

Carol handed Mama Gravy her beret. "I won't need this money."

"Money? In there?"

"Sure. Why do you think I wouldn't part with my hat? Why do you think I even wore it out on the town at night when you're only supposed to wear hats during the day? I sewed money in it to hide it. Not all of it - but most."

Mama Gravy asked, "Where'd you come across money? Your rotten husband?"

"Yep. How do you think I could afford to take us to all those movies? And the popcorn and RC? That ain't cheap. Here's most of the cash left from when I sold Antonio's car. And there's a new compact of rouge."

"A car? A whole car? That much? You had all this money all this time and you never shared it?"

Carol said, "I shared it some. But I also needed to save for the future. The future always takes money. But that don't matter now. I won't need things, being a nun. You take it." Carol clicked open her purse and added to it the jewelry she was wearing. She handed it over. "You can take all this, too."

Even though Mama Gravy had such riches, she frowned. "So this is a final goodbye. You mean it? You're not just saying it?"

Carol said, "Yes. I'm gong to the convent. I really do have to. I just can't keep living like this."

"A real big arrow in my heart goodbye."

Carol looked at her oddly. "Sure. I guess so. I gotta move on."

Mama Gravy moaned. "Ooooh, I feel old. At your age I was always skipping around, too, like nothing mattered at all. I just came and went like it didn't mean anything to anybody else. I didn't think about anybody else. But that was the 20s. You weren't supposed to think about anybody else. The Great Depression has made everybody have to stop and think about everybody else. But I guess it don't matter. You're still so young and life is just a big wide sky."

Carol grabbed her arm. "Don't cry. I think the world of you. You know that. But I have to move on. I'll visit. Sure. You'll see me again. It's a small world. And you were a wonderful stepping stone for me to help start me off in my life."

"A stepping stone! Just step on my head! That's what I was. A thing to step on?"

"I said that wrong. You were a full length yellow brick road."

Mama Gravy still wept, but also laughed. "I'm a yellow brick road! And damn was that road yellow, thank you Technicolor!"

Carol gave her a kiss on the lips. "You're my favorite person so far in my life. You'll see me around. I won't go up in a puff of smoke. I'll be out and about. You'll see me out doing nun things. I'll never forget you. And you better never forget me. I just gave you lots of dough, and that jewelry wasn't too shabby, either."

Mama Gravy asked, "Can I have your pocket watch?"

"No. A nun has to know what time it is, probably."

Mama Gravy returned Carol's kiss. She laughed very loud and then hopped off the streetcar and ran into the night.

Then Carol looked at the time and began to tremble. "What have I done? Have I sold myself short? I have sold my self short! I need to be a star. I need to use every last chance. I need to not give up until there's nothing left to give up for. I need to try and try again or I'll always live in doubt. I need to be a star at all costs or I'll never forgive myself!"

She thought and thought until she decided to sell her soul to the Devil, since that was probably how most stars did it, since talent didn't seem to be a main factor, and looks were dime a dozen. She resolutely got off the streetcar and thumbed a few rides to the desert north of the Hollywood hills, jumped out at a crossroads that was unmarked, and waited until the eerie moonlight came out from behind a cloud. The wan light allowed her to read her pocket watch. It was midnight.

"Devil! Devil! Devil! You! Come on out," she stubbornly yelled in all directions. "You're going to make me a star, goddam you! And I don't mean at poverty row. No - MGM! Paramount! I'll even settle for a King Kong sequel at RKO, Radio-Keith-Orpheum, in all it's Tinsel Town glory, yes, to be in a picture with Fred Astaire would be so swell. Now come out. Don't be afraid of me. I sure ain't afraid of you. If I can survive Mama Caltanisseta's evil eye and tealeaves, I can sure survive you. I survived six whoopee crazed brothers. I survived Mama Gravy going south on me. I survive anything."

She listened to the dry wind for a while.

"Aw, come on. I want to be a star and you're being a pill right now! Devil! Devil! Damn you! Come out!"

Carol got a sinking feeling. Maybe she was too unworthy. "I ain't such a bad girl that you already got my soul already. Do you? How dare you! You're a cad! I'm a good girl, I am, worthy of taking! I am not a bad girl!"

She shivered. Maybe she was already too bad to have anything to bargain with. She yelled for the Devil a few minutes longer and then sadly started walking back to town, feeling like she was out of options and she should just go up the backside of the Hollywoodland sign and climb to the top and jump. She wouldn't be the first to fall to her death over broken dreams.

She walked until morning and then hitched a ride into West Hollywood, so missed the sign. She hopped the first streetcar she crossed but wasn't sure where she was going.

Then Carol saw a welcome face get on board. "Oh! Sister Agatha of the Streetcar! Sit next to me! I'm so glad to see you right now! How have you been? What have you been doing?"

"How have you been?" the nun sat next to Carol.

"Not to well. Making a fool of myself thinking about suicide and joining forces with the Devil. What stupid things to think about. I feel so stupid now, by the light of day, that I just can't even believe myself."

"The nighttime of the soul happens sometimes. I'm glad to see you're feeling better, now."

Carol asked, "What have you been doing? Well, I hope. You deserve to be well. And you look so bright in the morning sun. You look like an angel. I'm so glad I know you. I need somebody to tell all my troubles to. I've been such trouble. Last night I was at the edge of the Mojave Desert at a crossroads yelling for the Devil to come make me a star. Isn't that horrible? I must have lost my mind. What was I thinking? I'm such a stupid person."

The nun shook her head. "No. The world is in far worse trouble on the other side of the planet. Your problems are nothing compared to theirs. I've been praying for Poland. Many souls are leaving this planet before their time and I must go there and help them find their way into the arms of Mary, for She is crying for them. The war is making many lost souls. Germany, Italy, and Japan have taken the world into the deepest of the valley of death. I must go to the lost souls tonight. I must show them the outstretched hands of Mary. The blue of her robes are as vast as the sky and can even hold all the souls of this new war. There is even enough room for all of Poland."

"Are you going to go on your broom?"

"Of course." They laughed. Then Sister Agatha of the Streetcar sized Carol up. "My. I must say. That's a very expensive gown. You have really done good."

Carol frowned. "Oh. It's just a dress."

"Such a dress signals to everybody that you have come a long way."

Carol agreed. "A long way down the wrong road. So far down it I don't know how to turn back."

"You'll have to think about that one. I can see your heart has turned into a box of coal. But that's what pretty clothes are for - to hide that - to hide our souls from other people. People look at you in your nice clothes and think you've made it."

"Yeah." Carol looked down at herself and had to agree. "I look real kipper, don't I?" She made a sad face. "Funny, huh? I'm the best dressed dame on the trolley, no offense."

The nun asked, "Made it to what? But I've read that beautiful things can now be made from coal; it's such a modern world. I read that they can somehow spin it into a powerful thread they call Nylon. It's used for fishing string, it's so strong. And for hose. They say nothing will make a lady's legs look better than this new Nylon."

"I heard about that, too."

The nun said, "That's kind of like how you are these days, huh. Pretty as a movie star's legs and tough as fishing string and it's all spun from coal."

Carol said, "I don't want to be like that. I just wanted to be a star. It was all I could think of being when I was on the farm, especially when I was locked in my little room. Now that all seems so stupid. I've been so stupid. I haven't acted like a real person at all. Real people can't live like how I've lived. How do real people live? How can I do that? What can I do?"

"I can only tell you to jump the labyrinth. But only you can decided what that labyrinth is, and what jumping it means – and how not to go from the frying pan to the fire."

Carol said, "I know what it means. I've been thinking about it ever since I met you so long ago, now. Do you think I could be a

Franciscan nun? A good one? The best? I want to do something and be the best."

The nun said, "It'd be hard for you in this town. In this country. Your life has been so out of balance that it would be very hard for you to find your center - your inner peace and quiet. But you can do anything you put your mind to."

"Yes I can."

"Anybody can. As long as they aren't mentally deficient, anybody can think up anything if they want to. People have thought their ways out of all sorts of deep holes. All sorts of people."

Carol asked, "Say a prayer for me. You're so good at that."

"Blessed are the poor in spirit, for theirs is the Kingdom of Heaven. Blessed are those who mourn, for they shall be comforted. Blessed are the meek, for they shall inherit the earth. Blessed are those who hunger and thirst for righteousness, for they shall be satisfied."

Carol pointed out the window. "Oh! There's the convent gates, already! I gotta go!" Carol blew a kiss and then hopped off the streetcar and ran all the way. She rang the bell. A few bored looking nuns came to the gate. "Let me in! I want to be a nun!"

One of them said, "And so does a bunch of other poor girls during a depression – especially during breakfast."

Carol stomped her foot in impatience. "No. Really. Let me in! I just gotta be a nun – I just gotta!"

"I can't let any girl in who thinks she wants to be a nun. It would be pure chaos in here if I did. If you need a place to sleep in our shelter, I'm sorry, but you'll have to try in the evening. And come early. It fills up fast. Come at about five. But no earlier."

"No! I want to be a nun. It's been decided."

More nuns gathered. "Decided by who? Did you have a vision? They all say that and then the first boy who comes along - and they change their minds about what their vision is."

Carol said, "No. I planned it with Sister Agatha of the streetcar."

The nuns suddenly didn't look bored anymore. "When did you

talk to her?"

Carol explained, "Just this morning. Just now. On my way here. On the streetcar. And off and on all year long, practically. She's always out and about at all hours of the day and night willing to talk to me."

"What did she look like?"

Carol said, "Oh, she was top shelf. Real aces. She wore white. It was so clean it glowed. In the morning sun I never saw her glow brighter. Like an angel. I wish I had her brand of soap."

A nun said, "That's impossible. She's been dead just over three years, now."

"That's not impossible!" Another nun chimed in. "It was her! A miracle! She said she would become an angel on her deathbed. Remember? We told her that angels were angels and people were people and they were two different creations, but she insisted that she'd return to shepherd people in a way she hadn't been able to before. Remember? She said it was because she'd been named Agatha at birth, and that name meant good in Greek. Remember? She said she'd always be good. Even after she died. She was special."

All the nuns grew became quiet as they thought about it, and remembered it. Then the nuns unlocked the gate and let Carol inside. They added, "In the afternoon, the Father will be here to take your confession."

* * * * *

Carol asked, while in the confession booth, "Where do I start? Tell me how to rank my sins, if I'm to go from worst to better, or better from worse, and know where to start. I murdered my husband. I then there's also kidnapping and prostitution and dope addiction and bank robbing. And I was greedy with my money but then I did end up giving it all to her anyway. I gave it all to my best girl friend who I made whoppee with so I can't be called greedy anymore. And did I mention I helped kidnap a nazi? But he drowned because the mobster I was with was such a dope he forgot to put on the parking break. The car rolled right into a swimming pool. So I think that sin should belong all to him. And then I tried real hard to sell my soul to the Devil so I could become a star, but he wouldn't show up, with me already being such a bad girl, I suppose. What a waste of time. The Devil can go to Hell for all I care. He isn't any good to anybody and I have no idea why God keeps him around. Oh, and I had planned to commit suicide but I as I walked back into town, I missed the Hollywoodland sign by a mile. I won't jump off just any sign. It's the Hollywoodland sign or nothing. Oh that sounds so horrible to hear myself say it now. You must think I'm insane. But I seemed to feel better with the sunrise and I'm all better now. Is suicide a sin? I can't remember that one. It doesn't matter anything I just said. I'm feeling much better now. You must think I'm insane but really it's just been a hard week. Year. Oh, I don't know how long, now. My whole life. All my brothers used to make whoopee to me every day, but I think that's all their sin. And Daddy killed the babies so I think that's his sin. Yeah. I think I've covered all the sins I can think of, off hand. I'll be a nun, now, and things will get better."

The priest was tired, so he took no time in talking Carol into turning herself in.

* * * * *

With a life sentence in prison, Carol decided she'd be a nun anyway. She put her wool blanket over her head and prayed for whatever the news of the day got her to think to pray about.

When Carol was moved to a new prison in the fifties, she pretended that she finally got to join a convent in Assisi. She pretended that she had learned Italian and began to pray in a language all her own. When she wasn't praying, she was a milkmaid on the Italian hillside and helped make very fine sheep and goat cheeses that they sold in the valley to raise money for the poor children. She died happy in the barn out back behind the tall row of poplar trees at the age of eighty-six with her sisters, herds, pets, Virgin Mary, and Saint Francis smiling down on her.

Visit StoneGarden.Net Publishing Online!

You can find us on the web at http://www.stonegarden.net!

News and Upcoming Titles

New titles and reader favorites are featured each month, along with information on our upcoming titles.

Author Info

Author bios, blogs and links to their personal websites.

Contests and Other Fun Stuff

Visit our forum and keep in touch with your favorite authors! Purchase autographed copies and more!

The newest horror classic from

Jennifer Caress

Perverted Realities (0-9765426-5-X-$5.99 US)

Sammy wants to be a cartoon character and live in the cartoon realm forever, but that isn't as easy as it sounds. One cartoon in particular will do whatever it takes to keep Sammy out for good.

Frankie is a paranormal buff. He and his friends investigate an abandoned insane asylum in the hopes of capturing ghostly activity on film, but not all of the asylum's residents are welcoming to the idea. In fact, some are down right mean about it.

Cree must carry out a dangerous plan already put into motion. When she disappears, Sammy and Frankie set out to find her and soon her mission becomes their mission.

StoneGarden.Net Publishing
3851 Cottonwood Dr., Danville, CA   94506

Please send me the StoneGarden.net Publishing book I have checked above. I am enclosing $_____ (check, money order for US residents only, VISA and Mastercard accepted—no currency or COD's). Please include the list price plus $3 per order to cover handling costs ($5 outside of the US). Prices and numbers are subject to change without notice. (Prices slightly higher in Canada.)

Name:_____

Address:_____

City:_____State:_____Zip:_____Country:_____

VISA/Mastercard:_____

Exp. Date and CVS Code:_____ /_____

Please allow 4-6 weeks for delivery.

Enjoy this psychological thriller from

Donovan Galway

The Calibos Factor (1-60076-016-3-$8.99 US)

Hale Whittaker was more than a genius. Through a revolutionary process, he could read and manipulate genetic strands like tinker toys. But when business and the military sought to profit by the worst possible applications of his discovery, Hale fought to deny them, even if it meant his own death. Power and profit were too strong a magnet, and his work was continued.

Hale did not stay gone. The world stood helpless as Hale contaminated the last of the Earth's fresh water with a serum known as the Calibos Factor, designed to alter genetic codes and transform the drinker into unnatural predators. In a world alone, human-kind must survive the Calibos Factor.

LaVergne, TN USA
05 January 2011
211315LV00001B/31/A